HIS FIVE STAND

A BEDROOM SECRETS SERIES

EMMA THORNE

CHAPTER 1

"Hey babe, I'm home," I called. With travel mug in one hand and a portfolio under my arm, I attempted to slip my house keys back into my purse and fumbled. Everything in my hands crashed onto the stone entryway of the condo.

"Fuck! Sorry! I meant to say fudge, or drat or something else!" I called down the hall scrambling to clean up my mess. Henry hated when I swore. My purse had toppled open, contents spilling; I chased a rolling tube of lip gloss, and then I saw it. My cell phone landed face down on the hard stone. I braced myself.

The face was . . . smashed.

"Son of a bitch, I mean beach," I muttered to myself. Staring at the cracked glass I couldn't help but think it was a sign from the universe; a metaphor that could not go unnoticed. Hey Callie, in case you haven't picked up on the shit show that is your career, you are having a really bad day.

Thanks Universe, I appreciate the sign. I wished I could flip off the universe.

My cell phone contract wasn't up for another six months. This butterfingers move was going to cost me a few hundred dollars that I could not afford.

"The firm got the design job," I said, slipping off my shoes and hanging my thin cardigan on a hook by the front door. "A $10 million project, top floor of the Smith Tower. Of course, Roxanne blamed me for the weather today, but she did use my designs even if she didn't tell the client they were mine. I knew they were mine and the client loved them. So there Roxanne you big meanie." I rounded the corner into the kitchen fiddling with my broken phone. "Have I mentioned yet how ready I am for our vacation . . . ?"

I glanced up to see Henry sitting at the kitchen bar beside Sophia, one of the paralegals from his office. Sunlight filtered into the kitchen from the floor to ceiling windows that faced downtown Seattle. There were two half empty glasses of red wine on the counter and their chairs were very close together.

"Oh, sorry," I said, feeling awkward and embarrassed in my own home which was stupid. "Hey Sophia, I apologize for my rant there." I smiled figuring if I didn't act embarrassed the situation might be less embarrassing.

It didn't help that Sophia was one of those beautiful pixie creatures with short blonde hair and bone structure so fine she could carry off any hair style. She radiated natural calm beauty.

I felt the exact opposite of calm natural beauty with my sweat stained silk tank and humidity styled wavy hair.

"You're home early," Henry said, standing. "Sophia was just leaving."

Henry was Sophia's mentor. They'd been spending late nights working on some legal briefs so I wasn't surprised to see her at the house, especially on a day that Henry worked from home. I just wouldn't have overshared about my day, and I was a little pissed at Henry for not giving me the heads up she was here.

"No, she's fine," I said, cheeks burning. "I just didn't realize you were both here. You should finish whatever you were working on, like briefs . . . or whatever." My voice trailed off as I wondered why there were no papers on the counter, no leather bound books, or no open laptops.

"I'll go," Sophia said standing. "I'm so sorry, Callie." Her voice dropped to almost a whisper.

"No need to apologize," I said, her comment confusing me. "Look my day sucked, you two can keep working. I'm going to get packed for our road trip." Then as if in slow motion, I caught a glance between them.

Sophia to Henry, their eyes met, and then dropped to the counter as she fumbled for her purse. Where was her briefcase anyway? Lawyers were always walking around with leather briefcases.

"No, it's best," she said. "I really need to go." That's when I noticed that Sophia wore a short skirt, a very, very short skirt and a white blouse that was rather transparent and quite inappropriate for work. She had to struggle to not flash her panties at me as she ran into the living room to pick up her sweater, which was on the rug in front of the fireplace. Her heels lay next to the couch. Why were her clothes strewn around the room?

My pulse roared in my ears.

"Holy shit, I mean shoot," I said, my head suddenly swimming with heat. "Is something going on here?" I asked, a strained smile crossing my face. My voice sounded oddly loud in my roaring head.

"Nothing is going on," Henry said, his voice deepening as he moved toward me. Sophia stood by the couch wide-eyed. She looked like a startled doe facing an oncoming car. "Let's not jump to conclusions without all the facts, Callie," Henry continued.

It was such a lawyerly thing to say, I was instantly annoyed.

As he stood there looking at me, I took in his unbuttoned golf shirt and casual jeans, he never wore casual clothes like this with work people. He changed whenever he had an appointment. He said it was part of his plan to make partner; he never missed an opportunity to impress his team. And yet here he stood in casual dress with little miss scantily clad. His cheeks flushed, his light brown hair ruffled. He looked messed up, he looked . . .

"Disheveled," I said, as Sophia brushed passed me mumbling some more awkward apologies as she headed to the door. "The facts are you look fucking disheveled." My voice rose.

"I'll call you Sophia," Henry called after her. "And there is no reason for profanity Cal."

"I disagree counselor," I said, eyes darting from the kitchen table to the rug in front of the fireplace. "Did you two just have sex in our living room? Please tell me this isn't what it looks like. Oh my God, I'm going to throw up." I looked at the deep shag rug that Henry and I had joked about breaking in when we purchased it from that high-end furniture store a year before and my stomach clenched.

We'd talked about it, but we had never made love on that rug. Not once. It suddenly felt like such a failure, such a horrible mistake to not have sex on that stupid shag carpet. But it wasn't like we had a bad sex life. We had a good sex life. A normal sex life. It was predictable, dependable, and sure we hadn't had sex in a couple of weeks but that was totally understandable. I'd been working late nights preparing sketches for the Smith Tower Penthouse and Henry . . . well Henry was always working because he was going to make partner and making partner took long hours and sacrifice. This was the deal. We both understood it.

It occurred to me that Henry hadn't answered me. I looked at him panicked. "You need to start talking and explain this. It doesn't look good Henry. Start talking. Start talking to me now before I freak the fuck out."

"You need to stop swearing."

"You know I swear when I get nervous. I'm working on it as a part of my personal growth plan!" I shouted as I paced in the kitchen clutching my arms across my body, and feeling queasy and cold with fear.

Henry exhaled audibly. "We did not have sex," Henry said, then in a softer voice. "I wouldn't do that to you, Callie. I would never have sex with another woman while we were committed to each other."

"Oh, thank God, thank you," I bent over clutching my belly. A wave of relief moved through me and my eyes flooded with tears. Half laughing and crying, I sat down at the counter where just that morning Henry and I had shared breakfast. He had given me a pep talk before the big presentation reminding me that I was paying my dues as a junior designer and my job right now was to stay below the radar and make the firm look good.

My coffee cup sat by the edge of the sink. I lived here. This was my home. This was our home. I suddenly felt very stupid and very emotional.

"I'm sorry, that was just so weird, the two of you," I laughed and ran my hands through my hair then covered my eyes. "I seriously thought you two just had sex. Crazy, right? I think I was projecting a bunch of work drama on you. I'm sorry, honey," I said, looking up at him. "I shouldn't have doubted you. Can we just open a bottle of wine and figure out which B&B we want to hit first on the coast tomorrow?"

I looked up to see Henry exhale and look at the ceiling, again. The tense look on his face chilled me. "You had reason to doubt me." He squinted his dark brown eyes as if speaking caused him pain.

"But you didn't have sex," I whispered, the knots returning to my stomach. "I don't understand . . ." I let my voice trail off because even as I said the words I knew it wasn't true. I did understand. I knew exactly what was coming next even if my heart and mind wanted to stay blind and dumb.

Henry sat down next to me and reached across the countertop to hold my hand. I let him. I wanted his touch. In fact, I wanted to go back in time and rewind the last fifteen minutes of my life. "Please don't do this," I whispered, feeling sick and weak. "Please, Henry."

"I was going to talk to you tonight," he said, his voice low and steady, his eyes locked on my face. "There is no good time for something like this Callie."

"Don't do this Henry," I repeated, hating the pleading tone of my voice unable to stop it. I had loved this man for five years. He was my world. We had plans, not just road trip plans for the week, but life plans. We were partners. We loved each other. I belonged with him here in this condo. I'd been with Henry for so long my brain could not imagine an alternate ending.

"Sophia and I didn't have sex, we have never had sex," Henry said, still holding my hand. "Sophia and I are in love."

CHAPTER 2

It is amazing how much two bottles of wine dulls a broken heart. My best friend, Cara—a certified therapist who is constantly on the lookout for poor self-medicating choices—had been the one who filled my glass that night . . . repeatedly. I felt better getting drunk with a therapist, it seemed slightly less pathetic.

"They're in love," I repeated for about the tenth time.

"Correction. They *think* they are in love," Cara said, sitting across from me in her PJ's, a blanket wrapped around her long legs. We had regressed to slumber party mode. Our hair in top ponytails, we were bundled in blankets drinking wine and eating handfuls of salty truffle popcorn.

"Well, Henry used to think he was in love with me."

I borrowed a pair of Cara's PJ's. They were too long on me since Cara was about five inches taller, but I'd rolled them up and they were super cozy with pictures of tiny troll babies all over them. Cara and I had been friends since third grade. She'd been with me through every twist and turn in my twenty-eight years of life. When my parents died the summer after high school, I'd lived with Cara and her mom. They were my support system in life. Cara was the closest thing to family that I had in this world.

"Henry and Sophia are in lust," Cara said. "Remember what it was like when you and Henry first got together?"

"Yes, I mean no," I said, as I wracked my brains for a lustful memory. We'd met at the Suzzalo Graduate Library. Henry had asked me out to dinner. We'd gone to a little Italian restaurant and I remembered thinking he was really handsome and seemed smart. We made out in his car and things had progressed in a really normal way. "I really don't . . . I mean we definitely had sex more in the beginning, but we were never out of control if that makes sense. Did you know they were going to have sex on the rug, on our shag rug?"

"You mentioned that," Cara said, sipping her chardonnay.

"The rug that we never did it on?" I took a big swallow of my wine knowing the tannins were going to kick my behind in the morning. Cara drank white; I drank red. I thought that was one of the reasons we were such good friends. We never had to argue over a bottle. "I should have insisted we fuck on that floor. I should have made him do me."

"But you know how Henry feels about profanity,"

Cara said, giggling.

"Oh right, I should have said something like Henry I think we should have sexual relations on our floor. I insist. Ravage me, right now."

Cara laughed so hard she almost choked on her wine. "I seriously cannot imagine what Henry would have done if you talked to him like that."

"We didn't talk during sex," I said, feeling suddenly self-conscious about our silent love making.

Cara raised an eyebrow.

"I mean we had good sex, it was satisfying. We just didn't need to talk which I think is very, very normal. It's normal right?"

"Sure, it's normal, totally," Cara said.

"We were good together. We had a routine, an understanding and it wasn't all fireworks, but we enjoyed each other and I thought he was the one for me, you know? I thought he was my one and only."

"I know honey," Cara got up and sat next to me on the couch leaning her head against my shoulder.

"Don't be nice to me, or I will cry," I said, tears filling my eyes.

"You deserve to cry sweetie," she said, kissing the top of my head. "You know you can stay here as long as you want. Josh won't mind."

"Um, that is going to be really awkward when you have sexual relations on your living room rug, am I right?"

"You're right, it would be quite awkward." She glanced around the room as if considering the logistics but then thinking better of it.

"Henry thinks I should move to Bellevue," I said, holding up a print out of a map decorated with yellow circles. Before I'd left the condo he'd handed me a manila envelope with details about dividing up our belongings, a summary of vacancy rates by neighborhood, and a check to help get myself established in a new apartment. I hated how the check felt like hush money or go-quietly-and-don't-make-a-scene-money.

"Bellevue," Cara snorted and pushed the bowl of truffle popcorn my way. "He's the one who should move to the other side of the lake. Screw him."

"But I am going to have to rent a place," I said. "Oh my God, I'm twenty-eight years old, single, and I have no clue how to rent an apartment. I'll need references, how will I get references? I've been with Henry for five years and before that was graduate housing."

"You have skills. You are a capable woman. You will figure this out," Cara said. "But, you don't need to figure this all out right now."

"I'm a capable assistant designer who designs and gets no credit," I said. My cheeks flushed at the memory of that day's disastrous but lucrative deal for the firm. "Roxanne showed my designs today as if they were hers . . . again. If I had any backbone I would do what I wanted and go into business for myself. It's just so hard to speak up sometimes. I should quit my job. Seriously why not? My love life is a train wreck; why don't I just go real big with a total life reboot."

"Easy tiger," Cara said, changing to her therapist voice. "You are going through a major life transition with Henry, take things one at a time."

"The thing is, I feel like I had a plan for my life and now I've got nothing. I'm off the rails," I said, tears filling my eyes and spilling over. Suddenly, I felt drunk and nauseous and stupid thinking of all the years I'd spent with Henry. "I thought he loved me."

"The question is: did you really love him?" Cara asked, her voice soft.

Once upon a time I thought I knew the answer to that question.

"I think you need to figure out what you really want, honey," Cara said. She leaned over and kissed my forehead

17

before standing. "I need sleep. You do too. You going to be okay with the blanket and the cat out here? There are extra pillows in the basket and drink more water."

"Yes, Mom," I said, stretching my legs out on the couch and pulling the blanket up to my chin.

"And if you need anything at all, you come upstairs and get me." Cara stood at the bottom of the stairs.

"I'm not bothering you anymore." Elsa, Cara's mildly obese Siamese cat, jumped into my lap purring and kneading. "See, Elsa loves me. Henry might not, but this cat freaking loves me."

"We all love you," Cara said, smiling. "You're going to be fine. You know that."

"I know that," I said, keeping a brave face but as soon as Cara padded up the stairs, I poured myself another big glass of wine. "You know what Elsa? I am not fine. I am absolutely not fine at all."

Elsa the cat stared at me with her unblinking, wide blue eyes. I tried to ignore the feeling that the universe had sent me yet another sign. In case I hadn't understood the broken cell phone metaphor, I was now a drunken woman talking to a cat. Thanks universe, message received. My life had officially jumped the shark.

CHAPTER 3

I woke that morning with Elsa the cat sleeping on my face and a headache that felt like an ice pick drilling above my left eye.

Hair in a knotted ponytail, red wine on my borrowed troll baby pajamas, I managed to down some water without vomiting though I thought my body might actually be happier if I got sick. According to the clock on the mantle, it was 10:00 a.m. I had a moment of panic about work before I remembered it was Saturday and I was officially on vacation. This sweet relief was followed by the sickening realization that my road trip with Henry was canceled because he was in love with Sophia, his radiant pixie paralegal. I wanted to cry.

Cara had left me a note in the kitchen telling me to stay all day, but I couldn't bear the thought of being alone and doing nothing. I stripped out of my sweaty borrowed PJ's and pulled on my skirt and blouse from the day before. I hadn't exactly left Henry's with a plan or an overnight bag. The truth was I hardly remembered leaving I'd been sobbing so hard. The memory filled me with equal parts grief and rage.

I wanted fresh clothes. I wanted my toothbrush and my good moisturizer. Once I had fresh clothes, I could hide out at Cara's and binge watch TV like a proper train wreck. It seemed like a solid plan.

The cab picked me up and I climbed inside wishing I'd dressed better for my get away. I shivered as a cold rain fell on the windshield. It was a damp and dismal day. The weather had gone from good to bad just like my life. I leaned back against the cracked vinyl seat of the cab, my fingers running over the smooth metal circle of my key ring and the key to Henry's condo.

He'd given that key to me five years ago. I remembered how he'd presented it as if it were an engagement ring even carrying me over the threshold as if we were a young married couple embarking on our life together. Except we hadn't gotten married and there was no ring; in fact, the condo was in his name alone. Sure we'd talked about refinancing and getting me on the title, but there were always numbers to run and nothing ever seemed to come of it. I had wanted to push for change but I always found a reason to avoid the conversation. I hadn't wanted to be a drama queen or cause conflict even though I wanted more.

I had thought we were happy.

His Five Night Stand

Great strategy, Cal. I thought to myself. Don't make waves; just let life steam roll you. How is that plan working for you?

Relationship officially off the tracks.

Career intact only because I'd gotten really good at keeping my mouth shut.

After five years of thinking I was building a life for myself, I suddenly felt like a total failure.

I held my throbbing forehead as techno music pumped through the cab. The driver nodded his head in sync with the drumbeat. It felt like additional punishment, physically and mentally. I caught a glimpse of myself in the rear view mirror.

Brown eyes, bloodshot and puffy. Check.

Sickly pallor to skin. Check.

In need of a shower. Check.

I'd pulled my thick brown hair into a pony tail and I wasn't hitting that messy-not-trying-too-hard-but-I-still-look-good mark. I looked like a disaster and I was pretty sure I smelled like red wine.

I cracked the window craving fresh air even if it was chilly. We drove through the university district, in stop and go traffic, finally making some progress and idling at an intersection.

Red light.

On the corner, a small thin woman with a pointy face stood in front of a brick building holding a string of blinking Christmas lights.

It was July in Seattle, nowhere near Christmas.

The cab idled at the light as the girl took the blinking, rainbow lights and wrapped them around a sign in front of a large square brick building.

The Holiday. VACANCY

The Holiday. It was such a beautiful name evoking images of exotic vacations abroad and fruity drinks on white sandy beaches.

The girl finished her wrapping. She had the lights going round the post of the sign like a candy cane and draping back and forth over the lettering. They were dim in the daylight but somehow managed to look cheerful in the rain, hopeful even. She looked up at me and smiled, her eyes meeting mine for a moment. I smiled back without thinking.

I felt something flutter in my belly. The girl's smile felt so warm, so welcoming, like the quiet glow of her lights. She looked pleased with her handiwork and the lights were clearly out of place. As I watched her walk inside, I felt this sudden urge to follow. I wanted to find out who lived in a world where Christmas lights made sense in July. Henry would have made some snide remark about her artsy nature, even called it tacky. I loved those irrational, beautiful lights.

"Stop the car," I whispered. The light changed and the cab rolled forward slowly. "Stop the car!" I shouted pounding on the back of the seat. "Stop!"

"Easy lady, easy," the cabbie pulled over in front of a church across the street. "I thought you were going downtown," he said, as I paid the fare.

"I was," I said. "But I don't live there anymore."

I walked out into the rain, the Christmas lights and a single word, Vacancy, drawing me forward like a magnet.

CHAPTER 4

I buzzed the manager and waited. At the sound of laughter, I turned to see a tall leggy woman with strawberry blonde hair walking up the path. She held the hand of a gorgeous guy with short dark hair and a five o'clock shadow. It was hard not to stare they were so beautiful together. The guy wore tight blue jeans and a thin white t-shirt that had been soaked by the rain—it was nearly transparent. The girl wore a pale pink dress that hugged her body and open toed sandals that looked completely inappropriate for the summer rain.

I felt incredibly self-conscious in my wrinkled blouse and skirt.

"You should have worn a jacket, Troy," the girl said, dragging the hot guy up the stairs onto the porch. "You look so hot in a suit."

We all stood huddled around the call box, I scooted over to make room. I really hoped I didn't smell like a wine bar.

"Less clothes, less bother," the guy said, wrapping his arm around the girl's waist. Right there in front of me, inches away from me actually, the man called Troy pulled this gorgeous woman close locking her into a passionate kiss. I leaned back to avoid bumping into them and could not help but notice the enormous bulge in the guy's pants. I flushed realizing I was staring at a stranger's crotch like some sort of a weirdo.

I looked away focusing on the blinking vacancy sign trying very hard to avoid staring. I even cleared my throat but the couple appeared not to hear me or care. They finally came up for air.

"Sorry," the flushed woman said, giving me an apologetic smile. "We haven't seen each other in a while."

"Twenty-four hours, twenty-four long hours," the guy said his hands never leaving the woman's body.

"No problem . . ." I said, unsure what I was supposed to say. This was what they acted like after twenty-four hours apart? I remembered one reunion with Henry after he'd been in London for two weeks. I think he may have kissed me in the parking lot at the airport which I had considered a good sign. I felt like such an idiot standing next to these two people who clearly couldn't keep their hands off of each other.

"You need inside the building?" the girl asked as she unlocked the door with jangling keys.

"I'm trying to get inside," the man said, rubbing up

against her backside.

"Behave," she said swatting at his hand, her green eyes not leaving mine. She mouthed the word "Sorry" and rolled her eyes as if we were girlfriends sharing an inside joke.

I was so on the outside of this joke. I had never ever had a guy all over me like that. I wondered what it would even feel like to be so turned on that I didn't care who saw. This beautiful couple was obviously going straight inside to have sex. I felt a little dizzy thinking about it. Sex. When was the last time I had been that excited to have sex? Had I ever been like that with Henry? It was also like 11:00 a.m. Did people actually just have sex in the middle of the day? Didn't they have chores to do, or errands and responsibilities, and all that other stuff that had kept me and Henry from being spontaneous for years?

I had a thousand questions but instead I said, "I'm here about the apartment." I nodded toward the vacancy sign.

"Come on in. I'll take you to Billie." The woman held open the door, the hot guy kept a firm hand on her waist, his hand moving along the back of her dress as I followed them inside.

"You should move in," the guy said, smiling at me as we walked down the hall. He had bright blue eyes and a dimple on his left cheek. It was hard not to stare at the cut of his six-pack through his wet t-shirt.

"I just started looking, but it seems like a very nice place."

"I can tell you'll fit in with the girls here. They all know how to have a good time." And then he winked.

Boom.

I actually stopped in my tracks for a moment. A wink. What did that mean? Did that mean I looked like I knew how to have a good time? And what exactly did he mean by a good time anyway? "Um . . ." I stuttered very uncertain of how to respond.

The woman swatted him in the chest. "Troy, would you leave her alone already?"

Down the hall a door opened and a short dark haired girl with serious curves turned to lock the door behind her. She wore a tight purple dress and gorgeous red heels. She had long eyelashes and a beautiful mouth that she'd painted harlot red. She looked ready to take whatever she wanted from whomever she pleased. "Hey Shea," the girl said to the blonde.

"Hey Bella, you have a date today?"

"Some afternoon delight," the curvy girl said grinning. "Looks like you've got your hands full too." She nodded at Troy before grinning and walking down the hall, her hips swaying. "Have fun Troy, but don't keep me up all night this time, all right? A girl needs her beauty sleep."

"You know I can't promise that Bella. You should join us, my offer stands," Troy said, his hands extended palms skyward.

I think my eyes about bugged out of my head. Shea, Troy, and Bella were so open about sex, about having it, and enjoying it. I had never talked like that to anyone, not even Cara. Was everyone in the world having great sex but me or was it just the girls in this building?

I thought of Henry and our love making. Sure I enjoyed it, but I could not remember the last time I'd looked at him the way Shea and Troy undressed each other with their eyes, or the last time I'd dolled myself up like Bella. She looked ready to tumble into bed.

I felt so lame in my rumpled work clothes. I had my reasons for my sad attire, but the truth was I hadn't thought about dressing up for myself or anyone else in a very long time.

Shea and Troy walked me down a flight of stairs to a door labeled manager. She knocked. "Billie . . . Billie the buzzer is broken. A nice girl here wants to move in. You should give her the apartment above me."

I liked Shea and the way she was rooting for me

without even knowing me. I felt like I was a candidate for an elite club instead of a prospective tenant.

"Hold on!" A woman responded inside.

I heard the sound of shuffling and the door opened revealing a slightly disheveled and flushed Billie. It was the girl I'd seen out front hanging the Christmas lights. A door closed behind her making me wonder if she had been alone.

"You're in good hands," Shea said. "I hope this place works out for you. Come on Troy," Shea said, taking his hand. "You've been a very patient boy."

"I have. I have been patient," he said, as they walked away. "I need some attention. Some one on one special attention."

"I know what you need, baby."

"Yeah you do."

I watched them walk down the hall together totally transfixed.

"So, you met Shea," Billie said, her voice a little louder than necessary shocking my attention away from Shea and her lover. Oh my God, I'd been staring. I hadn't even realized it.

"Yes, Shea," I said, stammering. "And we ran into someone named Bella."

"Oh, yes Bella. You ever need someone cursed, she's your girl," Billie laughed. "And Shea and Troy are totally in love when they aren't fighting, but really I think they fight for the makeup sex. You know how that is." She gave me a knowing smile as she took a seat behind her desk.

"Yeah," I laughed. "I know how that is." I did not. I did not know how that was. Henry and I never fought. We agreed. We got along. We never had fiery battles that resulted in us tearing off our clothes to makeup. Outside of breaking up we were very compatible.

I took a seat on a small red velvet couch in front of Billie's desk. The manager's office was unusual antique furniture, lavender walls, and a strand of plastic chili pepper lights draped along the back wall.

"I've managed this building for five years," Billie said. "The building has a mix of large one and two bedrooms and a couple of studios. It's funny, but right now we primarily have women tenants. It's kind of a girl's club. I have one studio available."

"A studio is great," I said, wondering how much space I needed and what did she mean by a girl's club? Were all the women in this building as sexy and gorgeous as Shea, Bella, and Billie? Billie lacked the oozing sexuality of the other girls, but she had strong features and deep brown eyes that stood out against her pale skin. There was a picture on the bookcase behind her of Billie and a tall African American man, their arms wrapped around each other. They were bundled up in parkas standing in a field of snow in front of a bank of trees. They looked like beautiful outdoor models having their picture taken in a catalog.

"You need to fill out an application," Billie said. "But that is really a formality. I can do a quick credit check and if you have a security deposit, first and last, we are good to go."

"Not a problem," I said, thinking of that damn check in the manila envelope. I wished I could turn Henry down, but my bank account told me I could not have that much pride. I promised myself that once I had the apartment I'd get on a budget and pay back every cent.

Cara reminded me that he owed me for my years of joint mortgage payments, but Henry had explained that was actually rent. What a prince, right?

"Have you been looking long?" Billie asked.

"Just today," I said. Billie looked a little surprised. "I just got out of a relationship. Yesterday actually. It's fresh and I'm ready for this, ready for a change . . ." My voice trailed off. I'd shared so much more than I intended.

"The Holiday is a great place for a new start," Billie

said, smiling at me. "And I like you, I think you'll fit in. Let's go look at the apartment."

CHAPTER 5

I followed Billie out of her office. There was no elevator in The Holiday, only wide carpet covered stairs. According to Billie, the laundry was in the basement and there were a few prized garages off the back alley.

"All garages are rented," she said. "People tend to move in here and stay. We haven't had a vacancy in over eighteen months."

I suddenly felt like I'd stumbled onto some exclusive hideaway. Thanks to Henry, I knew vacancy rates were low in the city. I wondered how he'd found the time to do so much online research in between work and trying not to sleep with Sophia.

We walked up two flights of stairs. There was one unit on the left side of the hall which clearly had to be a large one or two bedroom. Two doors on the right, 302 and 304.

"It's this one," Billie said, sorting through her keys. "304." As she fiddled with the keys someone opened the unit next door.

A tall guy wearing a black t-shirt and jeans stepped outside and turned to lock the door. He smiled as he glanced at Billie and me. I swallowed, my mouth immediately dry. This guy was jaw-droppingly gorgeous. He had wavy dark brown hair almost black, a strong jaw, and these amazing pale blue eyes that jumped out against his olive skin tone. He had broad shoulders, and strong biceps. When he turned away, I couldn't help but notice that his backside was just as gorgeous. I had to remind myself not to stare again.

"Oh, that's Theo," Billie said to me softly. "Hey Theo!" she called a little louder. "New tenant, Callie. You should say hello. You two might be neighbors." Her voice was a little sing-song as she fiddled with her keys.

"Oh, I don't want to interrupt him," I said, wishing I had bothered to brush my hair that morning. I didn't even have on mascara since I'd cried it all off the night before.

Theo strode toward us smiling. His pale blue eyes were even more magnetic close up.

He held out his hand. "Pleased to meet you, Callie, or shall I say neighbor," he gave my hand a firm squeeze. His voice had a lilt to it, British I assumed, though I'd never been really good with accents outside of knowing they made me melt.

His hands were large, strong and warm. I immediately liked the feeling of his skin against mine.

"Maybe neighbor," I said, laughing as my cheeks

burned. "I need to apply and see the place, but it seems nice. Like everyone I've met seems wonderful and so welcoming . . ."

His hair was slightly long so it hung in waves not quite hitting his shoulder or falling into his eyes. I had to fight the urge to reach out and brush the curls off his forehead. "Oh, you'll like it here," Theo said. "Billie runs a tight ship. Nothing but the most beautiful apartments this side of the University. Right Billie?"

"Got it!" Billie said holding up a key. I doubted she'd been listening to us at all. She'd fiddled with a series of keys before hitting pay dirt. "Almost thought I'd have to leave you here with Theo and who knows where that would lead."

"Who knows?" he said, grinning at me.

"Right," I said, smiling back thinking that being alone with Theo was not a horrible thought, not a horrible thought at all.

Billie opened the door and gestured for me to follow.

"I'll leave you two to your tour then," Theo said, nodding. "Later neighbor." He turned and glanced back once with a smile before he walked down the hall.

"Bye," I said, almost under my breath.

"Theo's great," Billie said, walking inside the

apartment. "He and Odessa live next door."

And Boom.

Odessa. Of course.

I allowed myself a momentary pang of disappointment and then let it go. Of course the beautiful man in the black jeans would have a girlfriend. Billie had said mostly women lived here. He was gorgeous and he belonged to someone else which was okay. The last thing I needed was to complicate my life with a fling, or a relationship, right? Right. Good chat.

"So, what do you think?" Billie said, walking across the room to open a window.

Apartment 304 was a large square room with light hardwood floors. There was a tiny tile bathroom off to the right, a small closet, and a tidy kitchen that faced the house next door. "The rooms are big, kitchen and bath are small but it's a pretty good space for a studio," Billie said.

I walked across the hardwood and tried to imagine myself living here. The windows were tall and high, walls freshly painted white with a forest green accent. It was so simple, so classic. So different than the black and silver modern lines of Henry's home, and the floor to ceiling windows that faced downtown.

He had a $1 million view, and this place faced an alley.

His Five Night Stand

His place was his, this could be mine.

I wanted it.

I wanted to live here with beautiful women who smiled and laughed and made out with men in broad daylight, and men who looked like Troy and Theo. Especially Theo. I wanted something different. I wanted this life.

"I'll take it," I said without hesitation.

"Great," Billie grinned. "When can you move in?"

"Today."

I wrote a check and Billie handed me a set of keys. I had found a place to call home.

CHAPTER 6

"This seems impulsive," Cara said, touring my apartment weaving between the few boxes she'd picked up for me that afternoon. "Did you even think about your commute? The neighborhood? Where will you grocery shop? I thought we agreed no rash decisions."

"It's a university crowd," I said, sitting on a folding chair that I'd picked up at the store. I planned to hit some of the thrift shops on the Ave., since I didn't want a piece of furniture from Henry. "And I've met some of my neighbors, they seem like girls who have fun. I think I could use some of that, fun, you know." I didn't mention Theo my extremely hot and unavailable neighbor. The last thing I needed was Cara lecturing me about emotional boundaries or allowing myself time and room to heal.

"I just don't know why you didn't rent a place closer to me, I told you there were vacancies next door. We could be within walking distance, meet at the lake for walks." Cara sat down on the floor, her long legs stretched out in front of her.

"I can still meet you," I said, not wanting to tell her that even though I loved her I wanted some space. I hadn't even realized I wanted space until I'd been given the chance.

I took a swig of my micro-brew, my freshly washed hair back in a ponytail. I'd traded in my sweaty work clothes for faux yoga gear and an old t-shirt that Henry hated. Cara had brought me a bag of clothes to get me through the week. I knew I looked like an overtired college student with no money. I wasn't a college student and I had no money, but at least I was being genuine. I wanted to be comfy and would apologize to no one.

"I know it seems impulsive but this place just felt good to me. I can't really explain it," I said. The truth was I could explain it but not in a rational way, so I didn't even try. This whole place glittered to me, from the lights outside to the people inside. I wanted to live in this shiny new world. Then another emotion moved through me, something closer to pride, but a feeling I couldn't put my finger on, not yet. "And its mine," I said, my voice catching.

"Oh honey, I'm sorry." Cara stood up and wrapped me in a hug. "I'm being selfish. I just wanted you closer to me. You have done more in twenty-four hours than most women could accomplish in weeks. Good for you."

She picked up her purse and slipped on her sandals. "I should go. You sure you don't want to sleep at my house tonight? You could skip the camping gear?"

I'd bought a sleeping bag and an inflatable mattress from the dollar bin at the store. I hoped it lasted the night. "Nope, I'm good," My voice caught again and I coughed to cover it up. I worried if Cara hugged me twice I'd fold. "I've got to face the night alone sometime, right?

She kissed my cheek and left.

I was struck by the tremendous silence of my new apartment.

"Shit, I mean shoot," I whispered, taking another swig of my beer.

I hadn't realized how much I feared this moment, being alone. I put away the take out boxes and rinsed out the bottles for recycling. I had the surreal feeling of being out of my own body, watching myself go through the motions of a life totally unfamiliar to me.

Where were the crystal martini glasses, the classical music in the background, and the gas fireplace? Henry was so particular about details. I'd gotten used to the way we were together but I found myself wondering how much of what had been us had been me at all. I took another swig from my bottle; a nice beer buzz moving through my body. This was something else Henry and I rarely did, drink too much.

His Five Night Stand

We drank expensive beverages from even more expensive glasses. And we never ever left our beer bottles stacked in a small pyramid in the corner of our kitchen. Never ever. Ever. I took the bottle and sat it next to the other two on the floor. It really wasn't a pyramid it was more of a line, and since I rarely drank I was smart enough to know that this was my limit or a little over my limit. I wasn't sure if I cared actually. Henry wasn't there to give me a disapproving look. I felt warm and happy, I felt good.

Looking at my stack of beer bottles I remembered how Henry always said things tasted better in crystal.

"I think things taste better when you aren't around!" I shouted to the empty room. "Ha! That's what I think you smug mother trucker." I muttered to myself laughing. My laughter came from deep inside fueled by a feeling of coming undone and a rolling beer buzz that was moving through my body at a ferocious rate.

I'd had more alcohol in 24 hours than I'd had in the past six months, and like any good drunk I was amazed at how good it felt to be tipsy and loose. I closed my eyes wishing I had someone to disappear into, a stranger to kiss, something dark and secret. How about Theo, the man with the dark hair who would never be mine? I wondered what went on between Theo and Odessa next door. Were they making love to each other right now? I wondered if Shea and Troy were in bed together. Had they stayed there all day? And Bella, had she found love this afternoon? Had Billie unlocked her bedroom door and invited someone back into her office? Maybe they'd fallen upon that red velvet couch.

Suddenly I heard the sound of thumping as if someone were pounding on my door or a shared wall. My heart raced in response and I had this thought that someone in the building was trying to get my attention. I'd been wondering about things that were not my business and this was a sign I'd been caught, but that was ridiculous. "Hello? Anyone home?" I giggled, looking around the room. I expected the noise to stop but the thumping continued.

Steady. Repetitive.

Thump. Thump. Thump. Thump.

I looked out the window thinking the noise was coming from the alley.

I followed the sound past the kitchen door, walking along my wall, one hand tracing the stucco, the other holding my cold beer.

Thump. Thump. Thump. Then I reached the point where the noise was loudest, right next to my closet. I put my hand on the wall and felt the rhythm vibrate beneath my fingertips.

And it struck me all at once. This wasn't random thumping, this was deliberate. This was intentional. This was a bed. A headboard, banging against my wall. I felt a wave of curiosity moving through me. This was Theo. This was the man next door.

Thump. Thump. Then ever so quietly a moan.

My mouth dry, breath shallow, I leaned in towards the wall and placed my ear against the wall.

"Ahhhh, ahhhhh." Then ever so softly. "Oh yes, oh yes, yes baby."

It was a woman's voice ragged and breathless followed by the low mutterings of her lover. The voice was deep and strong. For a moment I pulled away from the wall, embarrassed. What was wrong with me? I had been thinking about sex from the moment I walked into this building. First I'd stared at a stranger's crotch and now I was eavesdropping on my nice, extremely hot neighbor.

Thinking about sex was one thing. I couldn't listen to something this private. But as I deliberated the thumping increased, and the moaning grew louder, more intense. It pulled me forward like a magnet. My breath grew shallow, my legs weakened and I pressed my body closer to the sound leaning into the stucco.

There, there, please baby, like that, just like that . . . she knew what she wanted and he answered.

Like that.

Just like that.

Harder.

Faster.

With every word I felt my body humming with energy, a slow wave of pleasure building as I listened. I could see Theo in my mind. His shirt off, I wondered what he was doing in that bed. His beautiful hands on this woman's body. I wanted to know. I wanted to feel this.

More.

"More," I whispered.

Please.

"Please," I whispered.

Now. Now. Now. The wave inside built as the woman's voice grew louder, she was commanding him and moaning until her voice turned into a shrieking and wailing so loud I jumped back away from the wall my heart pounding, my bottle dropping with a huge BANG on the floor.

And . . . silence.

My pulse roared in my ears. I felt like a kid caught stealing from a candy dish. Shit. Had they heard me? Did they know I'd been eavesdropping? My cheeks burned. What was wrong with me? I wasn't some sort of a voyeur, was I? I was a normal woman who had a very normal sex life. I grabbed some paper towels and wiped up the spilled beer, trying to walk quietly.

The room next door grew silent. I slipped off the lights and climbed into my sleeping bag still thinking about sex. Sex. I liked sex. At least I thought I did. Henry and I had sex, we had for years. He'd been my second lover when I was twenty-two years old.

Cara said I was a late bloomer, I didn't feel late. I just didn't have a lot of experience having sex with people outside of a relationship, outside of Henry. What had drawn me to Henry anyway? Had it been his confidence, his kindness? I felt foolish and sentimental thinking about those early days. When we'd first started dating, sex had been a little wilder, not really in what we did; in fact, we always did the same things, more in frequency. I remembered one night we'd had sex twice and then again in the morning. I had experience, right? We'd even tried a few different positions, I could think of at least three.

And I came. Henry had pleased me, not all the time, but often enough. I closed my eyes trying to remember the last time we'd been together. Had I come? Had I felt that incredible shaking and shuddering? Why couldn't I remember the details?

My body rippled with heat remembering the sounds from the bedroom next door. I didn't need to go through my memory banks to know that I had never ever screamed or called out like that in my whole life.

In fact, I thought back to all the times I'd made love to Henry and I remembered that I was always silent. The thought made me sad and slightly more embarrassed.

What was happening in the apartment next door? What was Theo doing to make a woman scream like that? I wanted to know.

* * * *

I had dreams that night. I found myself walking the halls of The Holiday wearing nothing but a man's white button down shirt. My legs were bare; I wore underwear and I was looking for someone. There was someone I needed.

I turned a corner and I felt a strong hand move across my body. A stranger pulled me onto the ground. I couldn't see his face, but I could smell his scent. He smelled like sex and his body was hot with sweat. He hovered above me not penetrating me, but I could feel his throbbing cock brush against my belly, my leg.

His Five Night Stand

I wasn't afraid.

I knew him.

He was the one I'd been searching for.

"Don't tease me," I whispered. "I want to feel you. I want you inside me."

I was dripping wet and my pussy ached, but he moved past my opening teasing me with his tip. His mouth on my nipples, his fingers playing with my clit I felt a wave of pleasure building between my legs.

This person, this faceless man explored me. It wasn't sex in a way I'd experienced with Henry, but in some ways it was more sexual than anything I'd ever felt before. I wasn't afraid I was aroused, excited. I felt an aching need that I'd never experienced.

I wanted this stranger.

I needed him.

His cock pressed between my legs flirting again with my wetness. His breath felt hot against my neck as his lips pressed against my skin. With my fingers on his backside, I tried to push him inside me, but he held his body taut and strong above me.

Then his mouth was against my ear; his voice was low and strong.

He whispered. "Tell me what you want."

Emma Thorne

I woke up as I came.

CHAPTER 7

The next morning, I awoke to a text from Henry on my broken phone. "You OK? You need anything from the condo?"

It seemed so appropriate to read his lame message through the shattered glass. My body tensed and I suddenly felt as though I couldn't breathe. Henry had no right to ask me normal questions anymore. And what did he want from me anyway? Assurances I hadn't spent the night sleeping in an alley? I knew Cara had told him I'd rented a place. She had refused to tell him where. Was he looking for forgiveness?

There certainly wasn't any of that going around in my heart.

My fingers poised on the phone as I struggled with what to do next. Seeing his name made me want to cry and vomit at the same time. The sick truth of it was that underneath all my anger there was a deep wound, a sadness that made me want to hit reply.

I missed Henry.

Henry the asshole I reminded myself. It didn't matter. We had been together five years. I missed the familiarity and easiness of us together.

"Don't be pathetic. Get a grip. Get a backbone," I chastised myself as I dressed my body still humming from the dream the night before. My big mission of the day was to get my cell phone repaired.

I reminded myself that a dream with a stranger had been more erotic than anything Henry and I had done in years. We had been so distant from each other toward the end. It had been weeks since we'd had sex and it was hardly surprising I'd found myself in the arms of some faceless stranger in my dreams.

I thought about telling Cara about the moaning next door, but I was so embarrassed by my behavior. The last thing I needed was to give Cara another reason to think I'd made a mistake getting a place of my own so quickly. Even worse I did not want to be psychoanalyzed and learn that I was some sort of a voyeur on the road to deviancy.

I checked myself in the mirror. Ponytail, white fitted tee, yoga pants, and tennis shoes. I wasn't a fashion plate, but I thought I looked respectable in that yoga-pants-wearing Seattle way. I had circles under my eyes and I still looked a little puffy from the drinking. I was definitely going to have to find a healthier outlet. Or was that the dirty dream a little voice whispered. You came in your sleep fantasizing about being fucked by a faceless man's fingers. Maybe that's what's keeping you up late at night you dirty girl.

Maybe I did need therapy.

I stepped out into the hall closing my door, just as the door next to me clicked shut.

I swallowed, my mouth dry, afraid to look but more afraid not to.

I looked up.

A beautiful woman with long black hair and honey colored skin smiled at me. "Good morning," she said. "Did you just move in?" She locked her door, which had a whole series of extra dead bolts that mine didn't.

"Yes, just recently."

Her green eyes twinkled as she smiled at me, her face revealing not a hint of shame. In fact, she looked luminous, satisfied. "I thought I heard some noises next door," she said. "Welcome to the building, I'm Odessa."

Odessa.

She was gorgeous, sexy, and amazing. She looked perfect for Theo and I felt incredibly guilty for spying on them.

"Callie," I said, holding out my hand hoping she couldn't read my mind. She'd heard noises? Had she heard my beer drop? Did she suspect I'd been eavesdropping on her sex fest?

And with that I shook Odessa's hand, her fingers covered with rings. She wore a purple linen coat and high strappy sandals. She was voluptuous and leggy and magnetic. I could see why Theo wanted to be with her. Beautiful people like them belonged together.

"So is it just you, or do you have a lover as well?" She said the word lover a little lower, her voice husky, a wicked grin crossing her face.

I coughed, half choking on my answer. "No, nope just me. No lover."

"That's a shame," she said, pouting. Then she tilted her head and looked at me with narrowing eyes. "You're on your own. You just broke up with someone."

It wasn't a question.

"Um . . . I . . ." I stammered.

"You were with him for years and now you have a broken heart."

Again, not a question.

I felt breathless and exposed as if I'd stumbled outside my apartment with no clothes on. "I did have a boyfriend, a fiancé actually, but there was no ring and we never set a date. It's over now . . ." I stammered, unsure why I was over sharing with this woman.

"Oh honey," she reached out and squeezed my arm. It was so bold and intimate but somehow it felt real. Her smile was genuine and her expression seemed to carry real concern. I inhaled sharply as a splash of tears filled my eyes.

"I'm sorry," I said, waving a free hand in front of my eyes. "It's just kind of fresh I guess. It's been a really hard few days."

"You are going to be all right," she said turning to face me square on. She took both my arms in hand and squeezed. "Girls like us don't just end up at The Holiday by accident. We end up here because this is a place to find love again."

"Really?" A part of me knew what she was saying sounded like madness, but another part of me surged with hope. This was a magical place wasn't it? I'd seen the lights outside and felt something in my core that told me I could call this place home.

"I'm kind of an expert at broken hearts," she said. "I know just what you need."

My heart hammered in my chest.

"I'm having a party tomorrow night," Odessa said. "You can meet the other girls. I'll send you the details."

The other girls. Was I really one of them? "Thanks," I said, standing still.

"And I'll get you set up with someone who can help you with that broken heart."

"Oh, I don't think I'm ready to be set up."

"Oh honey, I'm not going to get you a marriage proposal, believe me." Odessa grinned. "Let's just say I've already got someone in mind for you. He is the best medicine in the world."

I was literally dumbstruck.

She walked away and then glanced back over her shoulder. "You heading out?" She held up her purse. I realized how dumb I looked standing outside my door, purse in hand like an idiot.

"Um, sorry. I forgot something," I said, trying to laugh it off. "Have a great day."

"See you tomorrow," she sang and disappeared down the stairs.

I went back inside my apartment and closed the door, leaning against the wood trying to catch my breath. The best medicine in the world. A man. She was talking about setting me up with a man. She certainly had experience sleeping with beautiful men. Theo oozed sex. I wondered what he looked like underneath all those clothes. He probably had a six-pack; he most definitely had a six-pack. A six-pack and an enormous . . . What was wrong with me? A few days in this new building and I was already sex-obsessed. This couldn't be healthy. Or maybe it was healthy. I felt totally unequipped to tell.

Even more complicated, talking to Odessa I felt like I had a secret. I was a spying school girl, peeking through a hole in the bathroom wall, listening through a crack in the door to things that were none of my business.

Odessa was so beautiful and confident and Theo was just about the sexiest man I'd ever set eyes on. Even if I couldn't say it out loud. I knew that I wanted to know their secrets. I wanted to understand what went on between the sheets in their bed. What makes her scream like that? I wished I could ask her.

And she wanted to set me up at her party.

I felt like a girl who had tumbled through the looking glass. What was I getting myself into?

CHAPTER 8

That night, Cara delivered a futon, a bunch of boxes, and clothes from the condo. Henry had been kind enough to pack up my things. I was relieved and annoyed by the gesture. Cara also brought a bag of groceries, cereal, yogurt, fruit, and told me I needed more in my fridge than micro brews. Cara stayed until about 9:00 p.m., and we spent most of the time making up stories about how Sophia would dump Henry someday. After she left I crawled into my slightly more proper bed and found myself listening and wondering.

What was that beautiful couple next door doing?

At 10:00 p.m. they started. I hesitated a moment since now I had faces to attach to both the voices. There was Odessa in bed with her lover, Theo. The beautiful man with the wavy dark hair.

I resisted for as long as I could. My whole body tingling, I slipped out of bed quietly this time, and padded across the floor towards the wall.

The bed, the banging, the moaning, it all seemed louder this time. I couldn't tell if it was my imagination but I felt as though the voices were coming through more than one wall, as if there were multiple beds in the other room. Odessa and Theo knew I lived here now. Wouldn't they be quieter this time knowing I was only one very thin wall away?

I ran my fingers up and down the stucco, growing wetter and weaker as I listened. What was wrong with me? I didn't do things like this. I'd never even watched pornography, and here I found myself craving the moaning and screaming of a couple I'd only said hello to.

I couldn't resist. I slipped my fingers inside my panties and pressed up against my clit moving in steady circles. I closed my eyes trying to imagine what they were doing together. Was Theo going down on her, his tongue pressing against her like my fingers? Was he inside her now?

The stranger's voice from my dream replayed in my mind. "Tell me what you want."

When had I ever asked Henry for anything in bed? I'd never ever asked for what I wanted. I was horrified to realize I wouldn't even know what to ask for. I'd never felt a need to ask or command. What did I really want out of a lover? I had no freaking idea.

But I knew what I wanted now. I wanted to come. I wanted to feel like Odessa on the other side of the wall.

My fingers moved faster, my body tensing, eyes

closed.

Odessa moaned. She sounded so free. I wondered what it would feel like to be unrestrained, uncontrolled, and wild.

My whole body tensed as my breath moved in rhythm with the sound of their lovemaking. Did they do the same thing every night or explore each anew? I wanted them to come. I wanted to hear it. I needed it. I craved it.

Their moaning grew louder; the sounds of the bed banging grew faster and stronger. I felt like a thief stealing someone else's pleasure, but I knew if I could hear them, if I could listen to the moment they came together, I could own it, store it deep inside myself and draw it out while I slept.

I wanted another dream with my stranger.

They moved faster and faster. My breath and movements matching their pace; my body tensing with anticipation, and my thighs clenching.

"Oh yes, baby," Odessa moaned. "More, just like that, I want more."

"Yes, oh yes," I whispered, my mouth open and body tense with pleasure as I rubbed faster and faster. I leaned my forehead against the stucco, my body sweaty, and my legs strong and pulsing with energy.

His Five Night Stand

"Yes please, oh god, yes," Odessa said, her voice moving higher and higher, my breathing moving with her. The energy building inside of me and spilling over in ripples and shakes as Odessa shrieked with pleasure. I leaned against the wall; my whole body shaking as an orgasm rocked through my body.

"Holy shit," I whispered as my legs buckled and the waves moved through me.

What was Theo doing to both of us? I sunk to the ground, spent. I felt wet, my nipples tingling, and body shaking. I knew I should feel ashamed, but I wanted it. I wanted to feel like her.

I felt like The Holiday was opening up doors in my mind and body that I had never even known existed. Was it wrong to unlock these feelings inside myself? I had just come while eavesdropping on the couple next door. It was like I'd somehow linked with the sexual energy, their pleasure reaching through the wall and straight between my legs.

In the silence I pulled myself to my feet, legs unsteady; I slipped back into bed, my cheeks burning again with shame but also something else that I couldn't express. It was more than pleasure . . . it was knowledge. I felt ashamed that I'd invaded Odessa and Theo's bedroom. I had no right to intrude, but I laid still and wished they would start again. As if feeling my need, the knocking began again against the wall, slower this time, languid, sensual.

I felt my body respond, growing wet and tense.

The moaning was lower and deeper and I realized that it was Theo this time. He was moaning and she was silent. I imagined that beautiful man stretched out on the bed, his light blue eyes locked on Odessa.

I heard a woman's voice murmuring. It was quiet, but strong and steady. It lacked the animalistic frenzy of before, but it was hot, controlled. Odessa was commanding him, making him hers. His groans came almost in response.

What was she asking of him? I sat up in bed, I could barely breathe. My legs so weak I didn't even move to the wall this time. I could hear them from my bed. My nightgown thin against my hardening nipples. I tried to resist but I couldn't. I closed my eyes, my fingers sliding down my body against my aching pussy. I touched myself as I tried to imagine what was happening behind their closed door.

I imagined Odessa on top of Theo. His chest glistening with sweat, his cock red and throbbing, craving her wetness. I imagined her teasing him with her tongue then straddling him, and riding him with her wet pussy up and down, pulling him closer and deeper. She would make him hers. He would grow bigger with every stroke. A throbbing heat radiating against the sides of her tightening walls, muscles clenching she would hold him tight, slowly and evenly pulling him deeper inside her than they'd ever gone before.

Their voices quickened, and she joined him moaning as the banging increased. I imagined him driving into her harder and faster until he couldn't take another minute and then he grabbed her backside driving deeper one last time. Her breasts bouncing above him, he'd arch his back and grab her tits as he finally exploded.

Odessa and Theo groaned together, the walls shaking as they climaxed.

I swallowed a moan as my back arched and I came again.

I lay still breathing wondering if they had heard me? Did they know they had reached through the wall and touched me? I felt like an addict. I needed this. I told myself it was the last time, but I knew I was lying.

I would listen and come again with them a thousand times if I could.

* * * *

The next morning, I made a run to a thrift store and got a small table, a green rug, and an unfinished bookshelf for my little apartment. I draped a pale green scarf over the table and found some shimmery white curtains that I hung in front of the windows. With the futon and cozy area rug, my apartment was feeling a little less pitiful and trending towards shabby chic.

I went for a run and took a shower that afternoon. Cara had invited me to join her and Josh for a movie and pizza, but I hated feeling like a third wheel.

Plus, you may have a date with the couple next door, a little voice inside me whispered. But since I'd heard nothing more from Odessa I wondered if her invite had been less genuine and more impulsive, or maybe the party was off.

At least I had a stack of books to read. Worst case I could hole up in my getting cuter by the minute apartment and have an appropriate amount of wine and a good read. There were worse things in the world.

I'd just stepped out of the shower when someone knocked on my door. I quickly grabbed a terry cloth robe, my hair wet and dripping down my back.

I looked through the peep hole.

Theo, the beautiful man with the wavy dark hair stood

outside my door.

Odessa's lover.

His broad shoulders stretched his thin black t-shirt in all the right places and his dark pants hugged his body in a way that made me want to step out of my robe. "Get a hold of yourself Callie . . ." I whispered to myself, taking a breath.

He knocked again. "Hello?" His voice was deep and had a timbre to it that made me feel a bit unsteady. I remembered his voice from our conversation in the hall and from his moans.

I cracked open the door. "Can I help you?" I asked.

I saw his pale blue eyes quickly move up and down my body. He didn't leer at me, or stare at a me in a way that made me uncomfortable, but it was very clear he'd seen me and it was even more clear that he knew I was naked. Somehow, having only a single layer of fabric between my damp body and me felt dangerous.

"Is this a good time, I can come back," he said, giving me a half smile, the lilt of his accent unbelievably charming. I would have listened to him read a dictionary. "I see you were in the shower."

"You are right," I said, "I'm all wet . . ." I blanched. "My hair and my body is wet I mean. Well not my body anymore, my body is drying, in my robe. It's a fine time . . . Shit. I mean shoot. I'm sorry, I'm Callie. We met briefly, but not officially."

"I'm Theo," he said, offering me his hand. "I officially live next door. We met . . ."

"I remember, yes, Theo," I said, my cheeks flushing red. I shook his hand, it was as large and warm as I remembered. He had a very strong grip. Theo. I swallowed, my throat dry. "I'm Callie. I'm new. And I already told you that."

"Yes you did," he said, his eyes crinkling when he smiled. "So, how do you like The Holiday? You glad you decided to stay?"

"I like it, it's been a few days, but it feels good here." Just saying the words "feels good" made me flush. Why did my every word seem loaded with sexual innuendo? Theo kept his eyes locked on mine. I had never seen someone look so focused when I spoke. "I moved here kind of impulsively, but I think I made a good decision."

"I think you did too," he said. "I knew you'd like it here. The women who live here are special."

"Special?"

"I don't know if you've noticed," he said. "But the women who live here are all very, very beautiful."

"Beautiful."

"You fit right in," he said, giving me a smile that was definitely tinged with a hint of wickedness. I couldn't speak. Was he flirting with me? I hoped he was and instantly berated myself. I did not want another woman's lover flirting with me. I had just been that woman. I was not about to mess with someone else's man.

"So, this is for you," he said, handing me a cream colored envelope, thick stationary. "Odessa likes things formal." He shrugged.

The paper felt expensive, I ran my thumb along an embossed letter O on the back. She had spent cash on this correspondence. "Thank you."

"We're having a party tonight. We'd like you to come," he said.

Too late, I already did. Multiple times. I thought, cheeks burning. Had he used the word come on purpose?

"Thanks," I whispered. "I think I'm free later but I'll have to check." Check with whom? Right. I sounded like someone trying to sound busy.

I had a sudden flash of Theo making love to Odessa and I felt this wave of jealousy and envy that was so intense I almost made a noise. I felt my chest tighten before a sound escaped my lips. He was not mine. This was madness and a fantasy. An addiction. An addiction that a smart girl would give up. A smart girl would never walk on the other side of that bedroom wall and she'd give up on her new found habit of invading other people's privacy.

But Theo was hot and I'd dated Henry for a ridiculously long time, and I'd come harder in this fantasy world than I ever had with Henry. Maybe it was time to start doing the opposite of my inner voice. I wasn't sure that little voice was so smart anyway.

"I'll hope to see you later then, neighbor," Theo said, grinning and with that he left my door. I stood there for a moment in my robe wondering how much of what he'd said had been casual conversation. He was on an errand from Odessa after all. His lover had told him to invite the new neighbor. And wasn't one of the cardinal rules of having a party to invite everyone who lives within earshot of your place? She had to invite me or risk noise complaints. For all she knew I was some nosy parker who'd call the police at a moment's notice.

No, you're a nosy girl who eavesdrops on their sex games every night, a little voice inside me whispered. And if you step foot inside their door you'll give yourself away.

I closed my apartment door and laid down on my futon opening the invitation.

His Five Night Stand

Please join us. Explore. Experiment. Enjoy. The games begin at 9:00 p.m.

9:00 p.m. And what exactly did they mean by games?

I held the thick white card running my fingertips over the slightly raised print. Explore. Experiment. Enjoy. Wasn't that exactly what I'd been doing from the moment I'd moved into this building?

My phone beeped. Cara following up to see what take-out she should order tonight.

I wrote back. *Feeling sick, going to read a book and go to bed early. Call you tomorrow.*

I got out of bed and opened my closet. I needed to find something to wear. I had plans.

What does a girl wear to a party hosted by a couple that has amazingly hot sex and has promised a night to "explore, experiment, and enjoy?"

I laid out a few different options on my bed. I'd worn a conservative and appropriate little black dress to so many of Henry's law functions. I'd dress it up or down with rhinestones or sexy stockings but the whole dress screamed I'm appropriate, I'm good. I didn't want to be good tonight. I wanted to be someone else, someone different. The sad thing was my wardrobe had been built on the principles of classiness. I didn't want to show up next door looking completely trashy, but I wanted something hot, something that wouldn't disappear into the walls.

I rejected two other dresses, a capped sleeve red dress that looked matronly, a navy blue strapless because it was navy. I tried on pants and a sequined halter. I had about given up when I remembered a red dress that Cara had bought and given to me because she'd bought the wrong size on sale. It was much too small for her.

Still in the bag in the back of my closet, I was amazed I'd held onto the dress. It was a stretchy satin that was normally about a size too small even for me, but since I'd been on a heartbreak diet, I slipped into the dress noticing the zipper on the side slid up just fine. It had a plunging neckline and a built in bustier that pushed my breasts up creating more cleavage than I thought possible.

I stood in front of the full-length mirror and slipped into a pair of silver sling back heels. Holding my hair up I piled it on top of my head into a loose bun, tendrils framing my face, then I let it down so my hair reached past my collar bone. It covered the straps of my dress. Definitely up.

Was it too much? I felt out of my body again standing in that red dress with those impractical shoes. Callie Barron didn't wear dresses like this. A dress like this looked made for drinks in dark corners—make out sessions against the wall. Both things I knew little about. It didn't look appropriate at all. Was it too much? Was I taking all of my own sex'd up fantasies and infusing them into Odessa's party? What if everyone showed up wearing jeans?

No. Odessa likes things formal. Theo had said as much.

I felt good in the dress. I felt sexy. I also felt like an imposter but if I was going to find the courage to walk into the apartment next door maybe I needed to wear a mask.

"Be someone else Callie," I whispered taking some red lipstick and painting it on my lips. "Just for a night. You can do this."

Before I put on the dress, I used my favorite citrus body lotion and slipped on a lacy black thong that still had the tags. I was happy the undies were new. I was tempted to burn every piece of underwear that had been on a wash and dry cycle in Henry's condo.

The dress hugged my body and with the thong there was no panty line unless you stared at my backside. I figured if anyone was staring they deserved to see.

I painted my toenails black. I didn't want to look too done up with red toes and nails. Remember I was going for sexy but not trying too hard which is incredibly hard to do.

I went through several different earring and necklace combos before picking thin gold drops and deciding to go without a necklace. I liked the way the dress framed my neck and collarbone. I wondered why I'd taken this dress and shoved it into the back of my closet. Suddenly I remembered Henry telling me it hugged my gut and looked a little slutty.

At 9:15 p.m. I was dressed. Hair pulled back, loose but not overly done. I didn't want it to look like I'd taken an hour to get ready, which I had. I'd redone my eye make up twice. The liquid liner had been a total disaster. Every eye shadow experiment seemed to end in the same smoky look but I finally landed on something that didn't look like a raccoon.

I spun in front of the mirror. Screw Henry and his opinion about my gut; the dress hugged my curves. I felt good. I felt hot.

The sound of voices and laughter bellowed in the hallway. I cracked the door open and peeked outside in time to see Shea and Troy standing in front of Odessa's door. Shea had her arms wrapped around Troy; he had a hand on her ass. Troy wore a black jacket and white button down and Shea a tight short green dress. It was hard to get a good look but I figured I'd hit the mark. This was not a t-shirt and jeans night.

I grabbed my key and slipped it inside the bodice of my dress; I had nowhere else to put it and didn't want to bring a purse.

I ran to my little kitchen and grabbed a bottle of red wine. "Never show up without a gift, right?" I took a deep breath as I walked into the hall and knocked on Odessa and Theo's door. It was time to go down the rabbit hole.

CHAPTER 9

I heard a series of locks clicking open and then Odessa answered the door. She held a simple white mask in front of her eyes on a stick bound with black ribbon. Her long black dress plunged down to her belly revealing the curve of her breasts and a long gold chain that held what looked to be a diamond ring.

"Neighbor!" She said, dropping the mask." I've been waiting for you, he's here."

He's here.

My heart rate skyrocketed. I felt a surge of adrenaline, something that felt like fight or flight. What was I getting myself into? Maybe this was a horrible mistake.

Odessa's deep brown eyes were lined with gold, her lips painted burgundy and her black hair pulled back into a sleek ponytail. She looked like a goddess. She raised her arms and pulled me into a tight hug before I could run. "I am going to make sure you meet everyone," she said. "Then we'll get you set up with your new friend." She raised her eyebrows. "You ready?"

"I'm not really sure," I stammered. "I brought wine."

She took the bottle. "Aren't you darling," she said

giving me a hug. "Now, come with me." The gold bracelets stacked on her arms jingled and jangled as she took me by the hand down a hardwood hallway into a large open room filled with people.

Music and conversation filled the room.

Odessa's apartment was decorated much too nicely for a brick apartment a block off University Avenue. It was a mix of antiques and modern, the furniture linear and spare, the carpets ornate and antique. I could tell at a glance the pieces were originals. I'd priced out rugs and paintings like these for clients. I began to wonder why someone who could afford furniture like this was living in an apartment one block up from the Ave.

There was a large crystal chandelier in the center of the room. The lights flickered, bulbs shaped like flames. The other unique piece was a series of empty birdcages hanging from what looked like a silver tree by the window. It was an extraordinary piece of art, an original I assumed. This wasn't some mass produced Swedish piece of style from Ikea. The room was twice as big as my apartment and I realized that this was one of the oversized two bedroom apartments that Billie had described.

Speaking of Billie, she lay on a long leather couch, her head in the lap of a beautiful African American man who stroked her cheek. He laughed and leaned down to kiss her sometimes holding a gold mask to his eyes.

"Aren't they beautiful," Odessa said, holding my arm. She leaned her head against mine. "I know you already met Billie. That's Vincent. He is delicious isn't he?"

"Very," I said, mouth dry as I swallowed.

"And do you like the theme?" She said. Turning she held her mask to her eyes. "It's a night in Venice. I always have a theme. I like to go places in my imagination. I think other people do too."

"You and your secrets," Shea said, walking past. "Hi Callie," she called over her shoulder, smiling. She looked gorgeous. Upon closer look the skirt of her green dress was shimmery and billowy but the bodice was tight. With her strawberry blonde hair, she looked luminous and ethereal. Troy stood beside her, his hand moving up and down her back as they talked. I wondered if he ever stopped touching her.

"So, you've met Shea," Odessa said. "She has a very interesting story. She comes from apple country. She's a farm girl at heart but can take on the biggest suit from Wall Street. That's how she met Troy but that's a long story, you have no idea."

She was right I had no idea.

His Five Night Stand

"And there is Bella," Odessa said, nodding at the curvy Italian I'd briefly met that first day in the hall. "Do not get on her bad side. She would take a bullet for any one of us. Once she gets to know you, she'll consider you part of our tribe. She was also engaged to a prince." Odessa sipped her drink. "I think there was some trouble with the law over that one, she'll tell you someday I'm sure."

"I only met her once, on the first day I arrived," I said. "We've said hello, no talk of princes."

Odessa reached out and grabbed Bella's arm. "Honey this is Callie, my neighbor. We are going to be the best of friends and you will love her too."

"Of course I will," Bella said. She stood on tip toes and took my face between her hands kissing me quickly on each cheek. I was pretty sure she'd left a red lipstick stain. "You'll be a good neighbor to Odessa. You know I lived next to her when I first moved in until I decided I needed a bit more ahem . . . how do I say this . . . peace and quiet."

"Oh please," Odessa said, rolling her eyes. "I am not a quiet woman at times. I hope it isn't bothering you."

"I haven't noticed," I said, feeling as though the ground beneath my feet had turned to a plate of very thin glass.

"And she's polite," Bella said, laughing. "No one lives

next door to this woman and doesn't hear her every moan . . . I mean word."

"I don't apologize for pleasure," Odessa said. "No woman should."

"I tease you, amore, because I love you," Bella said. "We all have a right to pleasure. Don't you agree Callie?"

"Absolutely," I said, suddenly wishing for a drink. These women had real lovers, I had an imagination and an increasingly concerning addiction to eavesdropping. I wondered if I'd made a mistake accepting the invitation. Maybe I was better off at pizza and movie night with Cara and Josh.

"Callie has a broken heart," Odessa said, pouting for dramatics and nodding in my direction.

"Madonna, no," Bella said, grasping my hand. "Where is the son-of-a-bitch? I'll tear his fucking throat out." She looked fierce, her black eyes throwing sparks. A vein throbbed in her forehead.

"He's not here, it's all right," I said, wanting to diffuse this tiny firecracker of a woman. "He doesn't matter. And I don't know if it's actually broken." Liar, liar pants on fire. My heart was in pieces.

"You look like it's broken, it's your eyes, they are so sad," Odessa said making me even more self-conscious.

"Did he betray you?" Bella said, her chest puffing up.

"Yes, well not officially, he showed restraint but he's probably done the deed by now." Why was I explaining so much to these women?

"Give me his name," Bella said, lowering her voice. "I know people. I'll have him cursed. Don't worry, it's not illegal, it's not murder, but it's very, very effective."

Odessa nodded, her face stone cold serious. "You should give her the name."

"I'm not so sure," I said, again feeling like I'd entered an alternate universe where curses might just reign true.

"She's not ready. It's okay, later," Bella said, nodding to Odessa. "Are you finding her someone . . . ?"

"Already done," Odessa said. "In five nights, she'll be just fine."

"Ah yes, five nights. You get your heart fixed, then you come see me," Bella said. "We will right all the wrongs in your world darling." Bella gave my hand a squeeze and then disappeared into the crowd of beautiful people.

"Isn't she just amazing," Odessa said. "Beautiful and powerful. She is a reminder to all women. We are strong."

"Absolutely," I said, wishing again for that missing drink, many of them actually. At least I'd worn my red dress, I would have been totally under dressed in jeans or god forbid my go-to little black dress with its matching sweater. If I didn't feel like I belonged, at least I was dressed the part. The women and the men here were all wearing tight clothing regardless of the shape of their bodies. Everyone sparkled and glimmered. They were radiant and oozed sexuality as they moved in circles to the steady beat of the DJ.

"Don't worry, you look beautiful," Odessa said, as if reading my mind. She wiggled her eyebrows suggestively. "You are going to feel so much better when he's through with you. Trust me."

When's he's through with me? My pulse quickened and I felt a surge of fear and excitement. What kind of heartbreak healing was she talking about here? I assumed she meant sex. That had to be what she meant, right? But I wasn't about to ask her like an idiot.

I scanned the room, nervous energy racing through my veins. I searched the faces unsure of what I was looking for, a familiar smile? A bolt of electricity shot through me as my eyes locked with a handsome stranger? That was idiotic. People fell in love over time, it took years to get to know people, accept their quirks. I knew that from Henry. He had told me once that it took years for him to love me, but he also assured me that meant our love would last forever.

And look how that turned out. Maybe you just need to fuck a stranger, a voice inside me whispered. You need to be more like Odessa, be free, let yourself feel something without thinking everything through for once.

"I think I need a drink," I said, feeling extremely thirsty and way too sober. I was well aware that I had been self-medicating a little too much lately but I felt entitled. I needed something to calm my nerves.

"Of course you do, honey." Odessa led me to a tall, gorgeous blonde woman and man who looked like twins. They stood behind a leather bar in the corner of the room. Odessa picked up a beautiful crystal martini glass and handed it to me.

"What is it?" I asked, not used to hard alcohol. "Do you have a cabernet?"

"Please. You are not drinking cabernet. This is a Sapphire Blue and it's exactly what you need," Odessa said. "Drink darling. Trust me."

I took a sip of the blue cocktail. It tasted sweet and sour at the same time with a splash of bitterness. It warmed my belly quickly and I found myself smiling a little more easily.

"I need to attend to some of my other guests. But why

don't you get comfortable, enjoy your drink. Watch the crowd," Odessa said. "It's the best way to begin."

"Begin what?" I asked.

Odessa just smiled and walked away.

I sat down on a large leather love seat that faced the couch where Billie lay with her beautiful partner. As they whispered and talked to each other he would lower his head and kiss her deeply and sweetly until it turned into something hungrier. I realized I was staring and looked away only to see Shea had Troy pressed up against a wall.

Music played, a mix of voices, sometimes men, sometimes women. I sat in my seat a warmth moving through my body with every sip of my Sapphire Blue, I realized I'd downed my drink in record time.

Bella stood on a table in the center of the room, a group of men and women had gathered around her. She held a mask in front of her eyes as she slowly twirled in beat with the music. Toying with the straps of her dress, she pretended to strip, raising her skirt as the rest of the people applauded until they turned to their partners to reciprocate. Men and women, women and women, men and men. Across from her a beautiful brown skinned man mirrored her moves, spinning in slow circles, his unbuttoned shirt revealing a taut muscular chest. They were so gorgeous, so sensual. I'd never seen a group of people so sexual, so free.

"Would you like another drink?" A low voice on my left made me jump though my reflexes were already a bit foggy.

Theo stood beside me offering me another Sapphire Blue with one hand; in the other he held a pint of beer. He wore black jeans again, and a black shirt unbuttoned just enough to make me curious. I wondered if he and Odessa had coordinated their outfits.

"May I join you?" he asked, his voice so charming, so totally irresistible.

"Yes please, to both," I said, accepting the drink and scooting over. Seeing him I felt a mix of attraction, jealousy, and relief. Attraction, because he was ridiculously hot; jealousy, because he was Odessa's lover; relief, because he clearly wasn't my heartbreak medicine. "Thank you," I said, taking a drink and wishing I was better at cocktail chatter.

"Are you enjoying the party?" He asked, turning to look at me. He took a drink from his beer. It was a simple question but I wasn't sure how to answer.

"I don't know. It's kind of strange here," I said, surprising myself by speaking the truth.

His eyes grew a little wider. "Interesting."

"It's beautiful, everyone here is actually. Is everyone you and Odessa know gorgeous?"

"Everyone here feels gorgeous, there is a difference."

I looked at the crowd and in that moment I understood. The men and women who looked so radiant to me, so sensual, their arms intertwined with each other. They danced, their bodies pressed together as if they were holding the most beautiful person in the world. Looking closer they weren't perfect, but clearly they felt perfect in the gaze of the other. I wished I had their courage. I felt beautiful when I crafted my look for hours. I felt a little embarrassed at how long it had taken me to get ready tonight. I wanted to look perfect and what did it get me? Nothing but anxiety. I had never danced with a man or woman the way these people moved together in public. Shea had turned from Troy and now pressed herself against a beautiful Asian woman. They slow danced while Troy watched until Shea turned back to him, her mouth opening to his kiss. She boldly ran her hand down his body lingering on his crotch.

"It's so different than my life," I whispered.

"Different from what?" Theo asked.

"I just broke up with someone," I said, horrified I was bringing Henry into this room, the blue liquid loosening my tongue, stripping away my costume. They say alcohol gives you courage, I think for me it removed my defenses. It was like my red dress and shoes melted with every sip. Watching these beautiful sexy people make out and pass masks around the room I felt like a frumpy girl wearing a sweater set. "I dated him for years, we were engaged well kind of engaged, there was no ring, or a date, but it was understood and then poof! We weren't and here I am. I have spent a lot of time at parties with men in suits and women in little black dresses."

"I like little black dresses." Theo shrugged.

"They didn't look like these black dresses," I said, as a leggy African American woman in a tight black dress with a thigh high slit walked by. "Is she a model?" I said, turning my head to watch her move across the room. "I think I've seen her in magazines."

"Maybe. Her name is Veronica; she stays with Odessa when she's in town. She models. She travels. I think she may be a spy, some sort of a government insider if you want to know the truth. It's hard to keep track."

"Are you serious?"

"Deadly."

I could not tell if he was kidding or not. "Well, you see what I mean? Everyone here is interesting and mysterious, you can tell just by looking at them."

"And you aren't?"

He caught me as I took another swig of my drink, I almost spit it out. "Me?"

"Everyone has a story if you take the time to listen." He had such a sweet smile and the way his blue eyes focused on me I suddenly felt like the only girl in the room. I also felt like an idiotic romantic, fresh off a heartbreak that I wanted to pretend didn't matter.

"Oh, I'm fine. I mean I have a story. I have a job. I work as a designer, an assistant designer, and I've done some interesting things, but I'm not interesting. I mean I don't have a self-esteem problem or anything, I'm just not flying in from France . . ."

"Flying in from France just means you spent a shit ton of time on an airplane. It doesn't mean you're interesting." I loved the way his eyes crinkled when he smiled, it was so joyful, so much sweetness wrapped in a package of total sex. He made me want to do a whole lot more than smile back. I seriously needed to pull myself together. This was another woman's boyfriend.

I took another swig of my drink trying to make more small talk. "So do you and Odessa throw parties like this all the time?" I said, louder than I intended, my words coming out faster without a filter. "Beautiful people making out, everyone looks like they are about to have sex." A couple stepped out of the bathroom together. "Like them, I think they just did, they just had sex. In a bathroom," I whispered.

"You are probably right," he said whispering back and then laughing. "I think a lot of people are going to have sex tonight."

"Well, I'm not," I said, taking another swig of my drink.

"Are you sure?" His smile was so playful, so flirtatious. It made me feel unsteady like the ground had tilted and slid my body a bit closer to him.

"Well, yeah," I said. "I don't know anyone. I mean everyone here knows everyone right and I just don't do that kind of thing."

"You don't have sex?" Again that smile, it was as if he knew my secrets.

"No, I have sex. Lots of sex. With people I know. You know, people who know me."

"Ah, so you have never made love to a stranger," he said, moving closer. He didn't touch me, his leg just a breath away from mine, I could feel the heat of him beside me as he looked me up and down. I felt a familiar wave of energy ripple through me. His eyes on my body. I felt my panties grow wet and that new but familiar aching between my legs.

"Do you?" I said, my drunken curiosity besting whatever good sense I had left." Do you make love to strangers?"'

"It's been known to happen," he said. He reached out and brushed a hair off of my face. "You mustn't forget that you are a beautiful woman too, just as beautiful as the people in this room. You deserve to make love to anyone you want, as often as you want. Tell me what you want Callie. You'll get it" He reached down and kissed me softly on the lips before standing. "I'll be back."

Holy Shit. Theo had just kissed me. Tell me what you want. Wasn't that what the stranger in my dream had whispered? And Theo had just kissed me. It wasn't a make out session but there had been lip to lip contact and it had felt good, it had felt very good.

But I knew the rules. You did not kiss another girl's boyfriend. Was I about to get myself rejected by the girls' club? I sat on the couch certain that my legs might buckle if I stood. The blonde fairy looking bartender passed with a tray of drinks and read my mind placing another one in front of me. My better judgement had departed with sapphire martini two, so I stupidly gulped this third drink down as a smarter part of my addled brain wondered if it was time to go home. The last thing I needed to do was be stumbling drunk in front of people I barely knew. I stood, a little unsteady on my feet, and walked towards the door. Odessa intercepted me.

"Well, what do you think?" she asked, her gold bracelet covered arm once again linking with mine.

"I think I should, go," I said. "I've had too much to drink." I took a step realizing I was more unsteady than I'd originally suspected.

"Theo will walk you then," she said.

"It's just next door," I said. "I'm sorry I can't stay."

"I insist," she said. Then she leaned over and whispered in my ear. "He'll know exactly what to do with your broken heart. Trust me."

Theo? He would know what to do with my broken heart? I wasn't sure if I was confused from the alcohol or the situation. My mind felt jumbled and drowsy and sexed up from the party.

"Just don't think too much," she said. She took my hand and passed it to Theo, who was suddenly beside us.

"Honey, take her home. Callie needs you." She kissed him on the cheek and walked away.

"I don't need you," I said. "I'm perfectly capable of walking . . ."

I swayed a little and Theo held out his arm. "You ready?"

"Ready for what?"

"Ready for me to help you home," he said, his pale blue eyes locking on mine. I found my eyes traveling to the cut of his shirt, his chest smooth, I wondered if he was smooth along his abs and in other places. I swallowed.

"Let me walk you to your apartment, Callie," he said. "I promise you, I won't bite, unless you ask me too."

"It is just next door," I said, looking into his pale blue eyes, uncertain how to interpret his comments.

"Then we probably won't get lost."

I slipped my arm inside his. "Home then, please," I added quickly. After all, I was nothing if not polite.

CHAPTER 10

As we walked down the hall, I remembered I'd hidden my key in my dress. "Can you turn around?" I asked Theo when we reached my door. He didn't even blink as I took a minute to fish that damn key out of my bodice. It had slipped down next to my right breast. I had to root around a bit until I could work it loose.

Finally, I unlocked the door.

"After you," Theo said. He held open the door and then switched on the overhead light as we walked inside.

"Not that one," I said, quickly flipping the switch. It was too bright, I felt exposed. I wanted to hide in the shadows. "The lamp instead," I said, eyes adjusting in the darkness. I walked across the room switching on a small lamp on my new antique table. It emitted a low warm yellow glow. Theo looked around my apartment and smiled. "I like what you've done with the place," he said. "You have a lovely eye."

Even with his compliment I was self-conscious of my draped silk scarves, crooked table, unfinished bookshelf. "I haven't really settled in yet," I said, my eyes drifting from Theo's gorgeous body to my futon in the corner of the room. Even though it was still set up like a couch, I was so aware of its functionality as a bed, I couldn't help but wonder what it would be like to fall onto the mattress with him. I realized I was staring. "I have more stuff, but I'm not sure if I want it anymore. Most of it's at Henry's, my stuff that is."

"Ah, Henry," Theo said, walking towards me. He stood close enough for me to wonder if he would reach out and take me in his arms, but he didn't. He just watched me with those beautiful blue eyes. "So, the foolish man who didn't know what he had has a name."

"Of course he has a name," I said, wishing we could stop talking about Henry. "He has a name and it should be asshole. He left me for his paralegal intern." I laughed a little too loud; I could feel the alcohol racing through my veins. It made me feel bold and uninhibited.

"You need water," Theo said, smiling at me. He took my hand, his thumb moving across the top of it as he walked me across the room to the futon. "You sit. And then you can tell me all your sad stories."

"My kitchen is a mess," I called, leaning back against the cushions. "And it's not a sad story, it's just something that happened. Something I let happen," I muttered. "After years of letting things happen all around me."

His Five Night Stand

Theo was back standing right in front of me.

"Your water my dear." He smiled holding a jam jar in his hand. "I couldn't find a proper glass."

I was suddenly very thirsty and getting sleepier by the minute. He sat down next to me and I leaned my head against his shoulder without even thinking.

"So, let me guess," he said. "You told me earlier that you loved him for years. You thought it was the real thing. And he cheated on you?" He leaned me back to see if he was reading the situation right.

"Am I that obvious," my cheeks burned. "Or did Odessa tell you?"

"No, but break ups usually include a betrayal of some sort."

Betrayal, the word sat on my tongue. Was this a betrayal of Odessa? Was I some drunk, horrible girl making the moves on another woman's boyfriend? I wasn't making the moves was I? We were just talking but he was holding my hand. Holding my hand and caressing it with those long gorgeous fingers.

"Did Henry make you happy?" he asked. I broke out in chills as he stroked my skin.

"I thought he did." I closed my eyes for a moment. "I like that. I like how you touch me."

"I like touching you."

My eyes snapped open. This was definitely flirting. "I don't think this is okay. I mean you and Odessa . . . I have heard you . . ."

"You've heard us?"

"I mean the walls are thin."

Theo laughed. "You heard someone else."

"Isn't Odessa . . . don't the two of you?"

"No," he said. "We tried to be lovers, a long time ago. It didn't work out and I moved into the other bedroom. That was over a year ago."

"Oh, so you aren't the one . . ." I said, my cheeks burning.

"The one she's been fucking lately," he laughed. "No, Odessa and I have not thought about each other like that for a long time."

"You did once, and you're still friends? That works out?" I said, mystified that a transition like that was possible and reeling from the information that he wasn't the one rocking Odessa's world every night.

"Odessa and I tried and we didn't work out. It's actually not that complicated. I want her to be happy. She wants me to be happy. She wants you to be happy and she thought we would enjoy each other." He shrugged. "So, here we are."

"You are her former lover and she sent you to me."

"Not her former lover and nobody sends me anywhere," he said, softly. "You are a very compelling woman, Callie."

"Compelling?" I laughed, snorting which slightly mortified me even in my drunken state. "I think you meant to say train wreck."

"You are extremely honest, very intuitive, and achingly sexy. I am trying very hard to not take advantage of you right now," he said, brushing my hair back. "You are very different from Odessa, but I can see why she thought we should spend time together."

"You want to take advantage of me?" I said, my mind latching onto his confession. I was suddenly aware of breathing, the very act of inhaling and exhaling made me think of my body and the parts of me that wanted to feel him on the inside. Oh my God, I wanted him.

"Your heartbreak is so pure and so honest," he said, tracing the line of my jaw with his fingers. "Odessa happens to know I have something that might help you." He shrugged and actually looked a little embarrassed. It was adorable and incredibly hot at the same time.

"What kind of thing," I asked, breathless, my mind

spinning and not from the alcohol.

"Five nights," he said, pulling me towards him. "I'm not what you'd call a commitment guy. But I love women and I love pleasing them."

"You love pleasing us," I said, unable to do more than parrot him. I wanted to say the words again and again.

"I've been told that five nights with me will heal a broken heart," he shrugged again. "It's not a guarantee, but it may be worth trying."

"What do we do these five nights?" I whispered.

"Do you want to find out?" he said, pulling me closer.

His question hung in the air between us. I could almost see the words written in front of me. Do you want to find out what makes a woman moan? Do you want to know what it's like to be impulsive and free? Do you want to take a chance with a beautiful stranger?

"Yes," I said, taking a breath. I felt like I was being offered the keys to a hidden kingdom. "I want to find out. Yes, please."

He leaned in and then ever so slowly he placed his lips against mine, softly at first his kisses fluttered against my mouth, his hands gripping me until he pressed harder and his tongue was inside me exploring.

I felt myself growing wet.

His Five Night Stand

Then he pulled away from me and rested his forehead against mine. "There are a few rules," he said. "Rules to protect you. And to protect me. Once we start this it's only five nights."

"Only five," I whispered. His hands on my thighs he had raised my red skirt ever so slightly, his fingers moving up my legs.

"After that we move on. I don't get attached, you don't get attached. We just please each other and enjoy each other. These boundaries are for you and for me."

"Uh huh," I murmured.

"There is the business of being safe in this world we live in," he said, his fingers tracing circles as he inched closer to my crotch. "I am tested regularly by my physician. I will show you the results and expect you will too."

"I'll show you mine if you show me yours," I giggled, resisting the urge to grab his hand and guide his fingers inside my panties.

"It isn't the sexiest part of our arrangement, but it's a requirement."

Theo leaned in, his lips against my neck "You are so fucking beautiful," he said, his voice husky. "Which is why I am going to go." He stood, suddenly and brushed his hands on his legs. I could tell from the large bulge in his black jeans that I wasn't the only one turned on.

"Where are you going?" I said, attempting to stand. I noticed that the room had started to spin a bit and I found myself suddenly sitting again.

"You need to sleep beautiful girl," Theo said, smiling. He slipped off my heels and helped me to my feet as he pulled the futon down to my make shift bed. He turned me around. "Is this okay?" He asked, his hand on my zipper.

"Uh huh," I said. He unzipped my dress. It wasn't until the dress was almost off that I remembered I didn't wear a bra. I grabbed my breasts self-consciously. Even my drunken mind recognized the irony in my bashfulness. I'd basically just agreed to get tested in preparation for some sort of five-night-filled sex fest, at least I thought that was what had happened. I was not entirely sure to be honest.

He laughed, "Do you have pajamas somewhere?"

"No, I mean yes." I brushed a hair off my face. "I'll sleep naked thank you."

"Excellent," he said. He laid down my comforter and raised it up as I slid under the covers wearing nothing but my panties. He turned away to give me privacy.

I must have looked hurt or embarrassed even though I was trying very hard to hide it. He was going to go home. Of course he should go home. I was a mess, but every time he touched me I felt a tremor deep inside. I wanted more. I wanted him.

"You know I want to stay," he said, tucking me in.

"You do?"

"The only reason I'm not is you need to sleep and I make it a rule to not take advantage of women when they are . . ." he hesitated and smiled as if choosing his words carefully. "Under a spell." His smile was so adorable and earnest I wanted to wrap my arms around his neck and pull him towards me. "I think it's important if we do this that you are completely present. Completely in agreement. I need to know that you want me with every part of your mind." He leaned in, his mouth against my ear and his voice low. "As much as I want you."

Then without a word, he took my hand and rubbed it across the bulge in is pants. He inhaled sharply as my hand moved over his hardness. He was rock solid and I was certain if my hand lingered I would feel his pulse throbbing through his jeans.

"I'll contact you tomorrow," he said, his eyes locking on me as he moved my hand back and forth over his pants. "I'll be back from the gallery around 6:00 p.m. Are you free in the evening?"

"Yes," I whispered.

Then his lips brushed across mine and settled on my forehead.

"Goodnight beautiful girl," he said. "I'll lock the door behind me."

And with that he stood, switched off the light, and left me almost naked in my bed. I couldn't move. I couldn't breathe. The steady thump of music next door suddenly seemed so loud. It appeared to me that talking to Theo I hadn't been aware of anyone but him. He would be home from the gallery after 6:00 p.m. The Gallery? What did he do? What was his last name? I literally knew nothing about him except he had once loved Odessa and had some magical bedroom talents for making women get over broken hearts.

And he has a really big cock, a voice inside me whispered. He will make you moan.

But I wasn't a moaner, I wasn't like that.

But what if you ask for what you want, the voice continued.

"I'm losing my mind," I said, closing my eyes. The sapphire blue cocktail overtaking me, I found myself drifting to sleep with the memory of Theo's hardness just millimeters away from my skin and the taste of his kiss.

Five nights.

His Five Night Stand

A five night stand.

Was I up for it? I'd never had a one night stand, let alone a five night one.

Would I give this man five nights?

Get over yourself, my inner voice said laughing. You'd give that man a hundred.

"Shut up," I whispered out loud as the spinning in the room increased. "I'm not desperate, I'm not weird, maybe one, maybe I'll start with one."

And with that I fell into a dreamless sleep.

CHAPTER 11

Sunlight streamed into the apartment. I hadn't closed the curtains. I woke up late with cotton in my mouth and a throbbing headache. My phone vibrated on the floor beside the futon.

"Hello," I answered, instantly wishing I'd had the good sense to let it go to voice mail.

"So, it's like a thirty-minute wait, but I put our name in for a table already."

It was Cara and she sounded very awake.

"A table? Where are you?" I could hear plates and dishes crashing in the background, and the hum of lively conversation.

"I'm at Boat Street for our girl's brunch? I sent you an email confirming yesterday . . ."

Drat. I had a vague memory of a brunch email from Cara, but I had been so focused on the party invite, I had forgotten all about it.

"Didn't forget. I just overslept." I did not want to go to brunch. I wanted to slide back under the covers and daydream about the sensation of Theo's hands flirting with the zipper of my dress

His Five Night Stand

"You weren't drinking alone, were you?" Cara said, her voice concerned. "You are not a drinker Callie and you sound hung over."

"No, I ended up going to a party next door," I said, standing. I felt better standing which seemed odd. I picked up a half full jam jar of water and sucked it down. "I had a cocktail. Okay maybe two, three if I count."

"You are totally hung over. You aren't bailing on me are you?"

I wanted to hide under the covers and pretend that my heart wasn't broken. I wanted to figure out whether I'd truly been propositioned by the hottest man I'd ever met in my life, or if that had been a drunken fantasy.

"I'm just so tired," I said, rubbing my temple.

"Come on, you know you want someone to feed you breakfast. You know it will be more fun than eating a sad piece of toast all alone in your apartment. Don't bail. Don't be that girl."

I folded. Cara had been too good to me. She didn't deserve to be stood up. "I'm in . . . I'll be there in twenty minutes," I said. "I'll grab a cab." I hopped across the floor pulling on a pair of yoga pants and grabbing a rumpled tee-shirt. I could sleep later. For now, something normal like brunch might do me some good.

* * * *

Cara already had a table at the Boat Street Cafe on their outdoor patio. She sat under a black and white striped umbrella waving as I walked down the brick pathway past the potted herbs the restaurant grew for their dishes.

"I already ordered coffee," she said, pouring me a cup from a silver carafe. "With half and half and real sugar cubes. I sensed you needed more than non-fat nonsense this morning." Henry was a fanatic about his fat intake. His condo had been a non-fat milk zone, something I had ranted about during our drunken break up. It was one of the many things that had bothered me for years that I'd literally swallowed without a word.

"You're an angel." I said, sitting down.

"You do look like shit."

"Thanks," I poured in cream, a lot of it. "We may need more of this stuff."

"So, what happened last night?" Cara said, her forehead wrinkling. I was definitely going to get her therapist third degree. "You didn't do anything foolish did you? You know how easy it would be to rebound in your current state."

"I did not do anything foolish, at least I don't think I did," I said, grateful for my sunglasses. I wanted to tell her about Theo, but his invitation seemed surreal in the light of day. I wasn't sure I could explain it in a way that sounded anything but insane.

The waitress, a small Asian girl with ponytails, dropped off some toast and jam sparing me from Cara's grilling for a moment. I ordered a hash with eggs over easy.

"So who did you meet? Are your neighbors, nice? Tell me everything." Cara said, taking a bite of toast her green eyes narrowing.

"I feel like this is an interrogation."

"Callie, I've known you since third grade and you're holding out on me somehow. You went to a party and clearly got drunk which is not something you do." Cara leaned on her elbows and lowered her voice. "You are still in shock over your break up with Henry, and I'm just worried about my best friend. I'm sorry if you think I'm being nosy."

"Fine," I said. "But promise me you won't get all judgey."

"I won't get judgey."

"Okay," I said again, taking a deep breath. "I went next door and it was a crazy party. Beautiful people dancing, everyone making out with each other. They were all so uninhibited."

"What does that mean, uninhibited? Were you at a sex party?" she whispered.

"No, not a sex party," I said. "At least I don't think so. Maybe a lot of people had sex, I don't know. They were nice people having fun, all consensual. And then this guy named Theo walked me home and tucked me into bed and . . ."

"He tucked you into bed." Cara's eyes bugged. "Callie . . ."

"Nothing happened, he was a perfect gentleman," I said, remembering how he had left after saying he wanted to stay. Had all that really happened?

"So, what did you do that you think was foolish?" Cara said, not letting me off the hook.

"Nothing. I just, I might see him again," I said. "That's all. And if I did, it wouldn't be a long term thing, I don't think he's into that, but I think I might enjoy him."

"Enjoy him," she said, eyebrow raised. "Are you sure this is a good idea?"

"Of course not," I said, taking another bite of toast.

The waitress delivered our food, Cara's egg white no cheese veggie omelet and my hash with eggs that were not over easy, they were rock hard. I prodded them with my fork.

"You should send those back," Cara said.

"No, it's fine," I said, taking a bite. Cara knew how much I hated making scenes especially at restaurants. I was notorious for never sending anything back.

"It's not what you ordered. You really should get what you want, Callie."

Her statement stunned me. "Tell me what you want." I replayed the voice of the stranger and Theo in my mind. Why didn't I think I deserved what I wanted? Why was I always more worried about conflict than my own needs?

There was a world out there that I had never experienced. People enjoying each other, exploring, moaning, and coming in the dark; people telling their lovers how to love them. People getting what they asked for, what they craved, what they needed. I wanted to explore this world, I wanted to stay down the rabbit hole at The Holiday and I wanted my egg yolks over easy dammit.

"Excuse me," I called to the waitress as she walked away. "These eggs are over done, this isn't what I ordered. I'd like to send them back."

"Oh, I'm so very sorry," she said, taking my plate. "We'll get you out a new order right away."

As she walked away, my heart pounded and I felt a rush of adrenaline move through my body.

Cara looked at me eyes wide.

I took a sip of my coffee and shrugged. "You were right. It's not what I ordered."

"What's this guy's name again?" Cara asked, eyes narrowing even more.

"Theo," I said, rolling his name across my tongue. "His name is Theo." I wondered where he was at that very moment. He had mentioned a gallery. Was he an artist? Did he work there? Did he volunteer? I knew virtually nothing about him besides the fact that I wanted him.

"I don't know what Theo did when he tucked you in last night. But I like this new you," Cara said, then she reached across the table and held my hand. "Just, promise me one thing. Be careful. I don't want you to get hurt."

"Oh, I don't think he's going to hurt me," I said, replaying the sensation of his hand on my zipper, his fingers on my skin as he shimmied me out of my dress. "At least not unless I ask him too." I raised my eyebrows and grinned.

"Man, I think I need to ask Josh to tuck me in tonight," Cara said. "I think I'm a little bit jealous."

That's when I decided.

I would find Theo and give him five nights. No strings attached. No questions asked. It was time to find out what would happen if I told a beautiful man exactly what I wanted and I wanted to start that night.

* * * *

There was a note under my door when I got home.

Night 1 - 8:15 p.m. T

It was the same thick card stock from the party. I held the invitation in my hand wondering if this was just an eccentric way to avoid giving me his phone number. Or maybe this was part of Theo's five night "thing." I wasn't naive, clearly he had done this before and I had to admit, so far he was good. I was intrigued.

CHAPTER 12

At 8:00 p.m., I sat on my bed wondering what to do next. I had on a simple black sundress and flip flops. Yoga pants and a t-shirt seemed way too informal and the dress from the night before was over the top. My hair was out of a ponytail I wore it brushed straight so it hung just below my shoulders. I wore a pair of pearl earrings and had dotted perfume behind my ears on impulse. I suddenly felt self-conscious and worried I smelled like a fragrance counter at a department store. What was I thinking? What if I had misunderstood Theo the night before, I certainly had been a bit inebriated. What if this was some weird drunken misunderstanding?

I stood up and straightened a picture of Cara and me that I'd placed on my antique table. Then I turned it face down. I arranged my shoes into two straight lines and impulsively decided to spray down the mirror and counter in the bathroom. I wiped down the sink for good measure.

Then Theo knocked.

I took a deep breath and opened the door.

Theo wore blue jeans this time and a short sleeved black shirt unbuttoned just enough to show the beginning of his chest. His hair wet he smelled like soap and spice.

He smiled when he saw me and I felt a fluttering deep in my belly. With just one look, he had me unsteady on my feet. Holy moly I hoped this wasn't a drunken misunderstanding. The man made me want to get naked.

"So, can I come inside?" he asked, when I didn't say anything.

"Shit . . . I mean shoot, of course, sorry." My pulse thundered in my ears. This whole asking for what I wanted was going to be really hard especially if I couldn't speak.

Theo took my hand as he walked in, holding my fingers with a confident pressure. "I'm really glad you were home," he said, again his voice low, his skin warm against mine. "I thought about you all day." The lilt of his accent was so charming; it almost seemed unfair that a man as beautiful as he was gifted a gorgeous voice to boot.

"I got your card," I said, nodding to the note. I'd left it on the mattress.

"Not too eccentric?"

"No phone?" I asked. "Is this a British thing?"

"Not British. Just no phone," he replied as if that were an answer. Then he reached for me and spun me around, his arm sliding along the back of my dress.

My pulse sky-rocketed and I couldn't help but giggle,

my body felt positively electric.

"You're very quiet," he said, his eyes searching mine for what, I wasn't sure.

"I don't know what to say," I blurted. He held me close, his hand moving up and down my back his face inches from mine.

"I can help you with that," he said, his hand moving to the front of my dress. "But first I need to know if you want this, if you want me. Last night we talked, but I want to know that you are choosing this."

"Five nights," I whispered. "That's the deal. I wasn't sure I remembered everything . . ."

"Five nights and nothing more," he said, moving away from me, his hand lingering on my waist. "It's important we agree to the terms. Five nights and then we move on. Do you agree?"

"I agree."

"And this is for you," he said, pulling a piece of paper out of his back pocket. I scanned the report, a medical summary of tests run and passed. The date was a week old.

"A healthy thirty-two-year-old male, 6'1", 195 pounds," I said, grinning. "Your cholesterol level is excellent."

"All right, I think you have the details you need." He

laughed taking the paper from me. "And you?"

"Right." I had managed to find my recent physical results in a box of files Cara had moved for me. I handed him the envelope. "I'm on the pill, and stamped and certified for approval. No diseases here." I laughed and rocked on my heels wishing I had found a way to make declaring myself disease free sexier.

He glanced at the paperwork. "Excellent pulse rate and cholesterol as well," he raised an eyebrow and grinned at me. "You are a healthy girl."

"Healthy as a horse." I blanched. "I mean not a horse, healthy as . . ." My mind failed me. "Can you just kiss me or something since this feels incredibly awkward right now? Make it stop."

A look of happiness and relief washed over his face. He took both my hands and backed me towards the stucco wall until I was leaning against it. I felt breathless and warm and I was aware that on the other side of this wall was Odessa's bedroom. Was I going to come tonight? This beautiful man wanted to pleasure me. I had never been propositioned like this and I'd certainly never imagined I'd say yes.

"I usually start slow the first night," he said, his mouth so close his lips brushed against mine. "But you can tell me what you want, when you want it."

"I'm okay with slow," I whispered as he traced a finger along my jaw down my neck lingering along my collar bone, and slowly moving to my cleavage. He untied one of the spaghetti straps of my dress. "You look very hot in this dress," he said. "So sweet, but sexy too, like you have dirty thoughts running through that amazing mind of yours. It turns me on. You look so strong."

"You think I look strong?" I asked my chest shaking as I breathed. Never in my life had I been called strong. My right breast exposed, he took his thumb and moved it across the mound of my breast lingering on my nipple. I could feel myself growing hard under his touch. He flicked back and forth rolling my nipple between his fingers. It felt electric, a flash of pain but this deep slow pleasure. I'd never been played with like this before.

"You are a woman, of course you are strong. Look at what you do to me," And again he took my hand and placed it between his legs. I could feel him hard and throbbing. I inhaled sharply.

"You have so much power. You can make me hard by looking at me, by allowing me to touch you. You are one of the most powerful forces in the world," he said, removing my hand smiling. "And tonight I want to savor you, I want to explore you." Then his mouth was against my throat, his tongue sliding over my skin. He untied the other side of my sundress as I stood pushed against the wall. My left breast exposed he played with my nipple just like the right until my tits were hard as rocks, then his mouth was on my right nipple, licking me, teasing me, then ever so slowly biting me as he pressed his body up against mine.

My legs grew weak. I had never known my breasts could be so sensitive. It felt like there were electrical currents running from my breasts to between my legs.

His tongue darting, Theo nibbled and kissed me until finally his mouth opened and he took my breast in his mouth. He was sucking hard, so hard my back arched and I pressed my pussy up against his crotch wanting to ride him.

"Tell me baby," he said. "I could play with you like this for hours. I'm going to make you come right here, just like this. Will you let me? Can I keep going?" He was breathless and intense.

"Yes, please," I whispered. I wasn't used to speaking, not like this, asking for what I wanted was harder than expected, but right now I needed Theo to keep touching me. I wanted to understand what I could do, what his mouth on me could make me feel. I felt an opening up inside of myself; I grew wetter, my body aching for more. I wanted him to fuck me with his lips, to consume me.

I felt energy building deep in my core as the wetness grew and our bodies pressed together. Then he stopped, breathing hard, he took my hands and placed them on either side of my breasts. "Keep them together," he said. "Please." Then he licked his finger slowly and slipped his wet fingers between my breasts. "Imagine me inside you," he whispered in my ear, then he lowered his mouth to my tits and sucked as his finger moved back and forth between my breasts, his crotch pressed against me. He just pressed he didn't rub against me, it was just this building pressure, the sucking, the pressing and then I felt the energy building inside me.

"Tell me what you want Callie," he whispered. "Tell me . . ."

"Harder, please," I said.

He sucked harder and pressed against my pussy as the energy grew until I was teetering on the edge of a place I'd never been.

I pressed his mouth against my breast as I felt myself falling forward, rippling and shaking as an orgasm rocked through my body; my legs buckled and he caught me in his arms and his mouth was on mine. He kissed me while the waves rippled through me.

"How did you do that?" I asked, gasping and shaking. "You made me come with my breasts and that pressure against me . . ." I struggled for the words. "How did you?"

"I didn't do that," he said, grinning. "You did. That was all you."

I felt dizzy and achy with a need I had never felt before. His arms around me still, I leaned back against the wall, my skirt on, my breasts exposed, Theo was still fully clothed. "What about you?" I said, feeling self-conscious. He had to have been with women who knew how to do things. I felt totally overwhelmed and out of my element. "I want to make sure you feel good too, what do you need?" I whispered.

"Don't worry about me tonight," he said, his smile breaking into a lazy grin. "My time will come, don't worry." He leaned in close his hands grasping the edge of my dress. "Night number one is about you. I have more planned for you."

"I don't know if I can come again," I said, I didn't want to disappoint him. I felt like I was in a new world and I wasn't sure of the rules. My body was in seriously uncharted waters.

"I don't think you know what you can do," he said, grinning. "Stay still," he said slipping my dress off my shoulders. It dropped to my feet. I stood in front of him in a pair of panties pressed against the wall. I felt exposed, but the way his blue eyes moved up and down my body I had never felt so wanted, so desired.

"You are so beautiful," he said, his voice low and his gaze moving up and down my body. He ran his hands from my neck over my breasts and to my pussy cupping me between my legs. He looked up; his eyes locking on mine with an intensity that made me feel unsteady. "Did you know that you make me want to fuck you a hundred different ways? That is how powerful you are."

He leaned in and kissed me. When we took a breath, Theo stepped away, his hand leaving my body I felt an ache as he moved away from me.

He unbuttoned his shirt as he watched me revealing his muscular chest. He had olive skin and what looked like a long scar across his belly. He moved to his pants, but I reached out and grabbed his hand.

"Let me," I said. "I want to feel you.

He nodded and closed his eyes as I unbuttoned his jeans. As each button on his fly opened I could feel his cock throbbing against the fabric. He did not want to be contained. I slid his jeans off slowly noticing how his breathing changed.

"I love watching you move," he said. "Watching you breathe."

He wore black athletic boxers his enormous cock pushing against the front. My fingers touched the waistband. "Not yet," he said, taking my hands. "We have five nights, love."

He led me toward the opened futon laying me on the mattress, my panties still on. "You want to come again beautiful girl?" he asked.

"Yes, please," I said, pulling his face towards me for a long intense kiss.

Then Theo rolled me onto my side, panties on he used his tongue on my ear, sucking and biting me while he pressed against my clit, never rubbing. I didn't feel like I was making out with a high school boy who couldn't figure out how to get me naked. This was erotic, and deliberate. "I'm going to keep your panties on tonight," he said.

"All right," I managed, my voice breathless and unsteady.

"I want to show you what your body can do with just the right touch."

I almost cried out as he sucked on my ear lobe and took

the palm of his hand and cupped me between my legs. His hand felt hot and he pressed against me as he bit down slowly on my ear, breathing against me, pressing harder and harder.

"You feel it building," he said. "I want you to think about your magnificent pussy and how I can't wait to stick my cock inside you. I am going to fuck you until I explode. I'm going to fill you up with every inch of myself."

And then I was almost coming again almost crying out but holding back, he slowed down and whispered "Hold it in, hold it in and breathe with me." I took a breath and felt the energy inside me ebb and flow. His hand against my pussy I felt my clit growing hard, I felt the power between my legs increasing, growing harder, stronger.

His fingers never penetrating me, I imagined my legs spreading, I thought of his dick above me, big and throbbing. As he pressed against me his mouth against my tits again, my legs wrapping around his body, his hard cock pressing up against me, not rubbing just that steady deliberate pressing. I wanted him. I craved the feeling of him driving inside me. I wanted more, I wanted to feel him inside me.

He brought me to the edge of coming, my breath growing deeper and more ragged. I didn't moan. I was afraid to let out the roar I felt inside. Holding onto my breath he left my pussy and crawled up my body, his mouth finding mine, his tongue sliding inside of me with a gentle hunger. I wrapped my legs around his body hooking myself against him. I could feel his cock against me hard and strong.

"You ready to come again baby," he said.

"Yes, please. Please."

"Tell me how this time."

"Tell you?" My voice almost squeaked.

"You choose. You are in charge. You can come with my mouth on your tits, I can suck you off. I can nibble on your ear and press against your pussy. I can suck on your fingers or your toes and play with your pussy or push my cock against you. You choose, love."

"I don't know."

"But you do know," he said, grinning devilishly. "I'm going to show you that you do know what you want. I want you to ask me."

"Your mouth," I said, my cheeks burning. "Will you put your mouth on my tits and press your cock against me."

"Of course," he said, his mouth moving down my body. "What do you imagine when I do this to you?"

"I imagine you . . ."

"What am I doing to you?" he said between kisses, his voice heavy his cock heavier against my skin.

"I imagine . . . I imagine your cock spreading me open, pushing inside me, filling me up."

"Fuck yes," He said. Burying his face into my tits, his cock throbbing against my pussy, I wrapped my legs around his body.

"Please more," I said. "Please."

"I can't hear what you want baby," he said. His mouth sucking against me, his hand on my clit moving in slow circles. "You want this." He moved faster in faster in circles.

"I want you to make me come," I said, my voice a whisper again.

"I can't hear you."

He rubbed faster, faster. I felt a building heat.

"Make me come. Please make me come."

"Louder baby, louder."

And as he sucked my tits, his hand rubbing against my clit, I arched my back and grabbed his body suddenly shaking and shuddering. I screamed as my body shook and shuddered, breathless I collapsed onto the bed, his hand still moving in slow circles. I whimpered as the orgasm slowed, then his lips on my tits he sucked as little ripples moved through me, then to my mouth.

"You just came three times in like thirty minutes," He said, his lips on my mouth, my cheeks, my closed eye lids.

"Three times? You mean twice."

"We aren't done yet."

"You must let me rest," I laughed enjoying the feeling of his arms around me, his body pressed up against mine, I could feel his hard cock pressing against me.

"But you are addictive, sweet Callie." He nibbled against my neck.

"But you haven't come yet," I said. "It's your turn." I rolled away and ran my hands down his belly tracing the line of hair that started at his belly button.

He smiled at me and interlaced his fingers in mine kissing my hand. "The first night, this is how it goes. I promise you, I am enjoying this."

I knew I wasn't supposed to ask questions but hearing him state that this was our first night together, it felt like a formula, a plan. Sure it was a plan I agreed to and so far I had no regrets but I was so curious. "So, is this something you do every time?" I asked softly, wondering if I was pressing my luck. "This is your first night plan. Is it a routine?"

"It's not a routine, it's never exactly the same, but I

have done this before," he said.

"With other women?"

"Of course with other women," he said, leaning over to kiss me. "Don't tell me you are going to get jealous."

"No," I said.

He pulled my comforter off the ground and covered us up.

"I remember the rules, five nights, nothing more," I said. My hands on his body, I felt my fingers brush against the scar across his belly. He bristled. "What happened to you here?"

"It was an accident," he said, his body tense. "It happened a long time ago."

"Sorry, I didn't mean to pry," I said.

"You aren't prying, it's just not why I'm here. I'm not here to tell you my sad stories."

"So, it's a sad story?"

"You'll get that much out of me," he said, smiling and rolling on top of me.

"Oh my God, I don't think I can do it again."

"We are not even naked Callie," he said. "And you are certainly not done coming tonight."

"I have had sex before you know," I said, playfully. He was right; I had never come like this with anyone.

"Oh, I know, and you will have sex with me," he said.

"I will?"

"Just not yet."

He rolled onto his back. "Climb on top of me," he said.

I rolled over and sat on top of him straddling his cock.

"Did you like how your pussy felt?" he asked.

"Yes."

"Show me what felt good. Make yourself come right here. I want to watch."

"You want to watch." My pulse raced with excitement and a huge dose of fear.

"Yes please, I want to watch you. Nothing is more erotic than a woman as she feels pleasure. You are gorgeous all the time, but watching you come, it blows my mind."

"I'm not sure I can do it," I whispered. "I'm not a prude or anything, I can make myself come, but I don't usually do that, especially not in front of people."

"I'm not people, I'm your lover," he said, rolling over he kissed me his tongue sliding inside my mouth, his hand resting against my pussy.

"You're my lover," I murmured the word thrilling me, making me even wetter.

"So, tell me what turns you on, lover, show me," he

said, moving his mouth to my neck.

I closed my eyes and inhaled deeply letting the heat between my legs paint a picture in my mind. I could see us, the way I wanted us to be. "I'm lying on the bed, with my legs spread," I whispered.

"Fuck yes, baby," He said, pressing his body next to me. I could feel his hardness.

I spread my legs and slid a hand down my body, slipping into my panties. I touched myself, one hand on my tits, the other between my legs. I moved in slow circles the way he had touched me, the way I'd touched myself when listening to the love making next door. "I'm thinking of your cock and how much I want you inside me," I said.

"Tell me more," he whispered, his mouth on my throat.

"I can't," I said, "I can't say it all." The words were failing me, I could see the pictures but it was so difficult to speak out loud.

"That's okay, that's okay, he said, "You're perfect love, just close your eyes and explore."

I rubbed my clit in slow circles remembering how he had touched me, I moved faster and harder thinking of him pressed against me wanting his cock inside me I arched my back wishing I could pull him inside, wishing he would fuck me. My fingers squeezing my tits harder and harder.

His Five Night Stand

"Touch me," I said, "Please touch me." I took his hand and placed it on my tits as I rubbed. "Harder, harder." My voice growing, he leaned in and whispered.

"I want to hear you moan baby."

And with that I screamed "Now, now, now," as he pinched me so hard, I felt a wave of pain and pleasure rock through me and my voice echoed off the walls.

We both slept. And I woke up alone. The clock said 1:00 a.m.

I closed my eyes wondering if the hours in bed with him had been a dream. We hadn't had sex but we had made love in a way I couldn't understand. I had never experienced something so erotic, so primal and his penis had never touched my bare skin. In some ways it had felt juvenile, like high school students afraid to take off their clothes, but in some ways it had felt more sexually charged than any of the nights I'd spent with Henry completely naked.

I woke up later that night to noises from the bedroom next door. It was 4:00 a.m. I sat up in bed my heart racing. I had screamed earlier, had Odessa heard me? There was moaning and the murmuring of conversation. I wondered who Odessa had in her bed tonight. Who had she chosen to love from that sea of beautiful people? "With your mouth,"

Odessa said, her voice clear and ragged with wanting. "Like that, with your mouth."

I lay down in bed my legs spread and imagined Theo's head between my legs. He had touched me in ways I had never been touched and I wanted more next time. I wanted his mouth, his tongue, I wanted him inside me. I didn't hesitate this time. I touched myself and let myself move with the moans next door and this time I didn't feel like an outsider. I was one of them. I was learning what made me come too. I felt the rippling as Odessa screamed. I imagined her holding a stranger's face against her pussy, his tongue inside her like a cock, she pressed against him as they fucked.

I came so hard I bit my lip.

CHAPTER 13

The next morning the memory of the night with Theo was confusing, sexy, embarrassing, and thrilling in that order. First I wanted to call him up and tell him that I wasn't the kind of girl who rolled around half naked with men I barely knew. Then I wanted to knock on his door and beg him to make me come again right that very moment, because I was absolutely the kind of girl who rolled around half naked with men I barely knew. This was followed by a sudden fear that I'd been too loud or too something mixed with an adrenaline rush that made me want to replay every delicious moment of our night together slowly, very slowly.

I had so many questions for Theo, so many questions for myself. I wanted to hear his beautiful deep voice assure me that the night we'd spent together had been as transformative for him as it was for me.

But there were rules.

Five nights. Nothing more.

No phones.

Fancy notecards.

And I'd agreed to the rules which meant he would

contact me, and I needed a plan for the day. I was a single woman and on my own.

This was technically the first day of my vacation. At this point Henry and I were supposed to be out on the Oregon Coast at a B&B in Seaside. Just thinking about the itinerary on the fridge made my stomach turn. Henry had planned out every stop. I wondered at what point in his planning did it occur to him he'd rather be sleeping with Sophia than me.

"Quit with the pity party Callie," I said, deciding the only reasonable thing was to get dressed and try to make something of my day. There were a few thrift stores on the Ave I wanted to hit. My apartment still lacked a real sense of style.

As I got dressed, I pushed Henry to the back of my mind and thought instead, of Theo and how he'd played with me with his hands, his mouth, and his cock. Every move designed to make me want more and it had worked. The start of the night I'd been almost too nervous to speak and by the end I had been screaming at the top of my lungs.

I stood in front of the mirror in my black and white tiled bathroom as I brushed my hair back into a ponytail. My cheeks flushed, I wondered if it was my imagination but I felt more alive this morning. Was my skin less pasty?

Did I look less sickly, less broken and sad?

Was Theo's promise to heal my broken heart in five days real?

Or, was I being played by a guy who just liked to fuck around with strangers?

The last thought made my stomach turn. We'd been safe, we hadn't even touched each other skin on skin yet and I'd seen his test results. I was on the pill and I wondered if we'd use a condom if and when we had sex. We probably should, the pill wasn't 100 percent; we'd swapped medical info, but it was never a bad idea to be too safe.

I had been with Henry for so long I wasn't used to these kinds of conversations or even internal debates. I'd have to talk with Theo about using more protection if things progressed. Still the idea of his skin against mine was so sexy. I hated to think of the thin skin of a condom between us, but wasn't that the type of stupid thinking that caused trouble? I was thinking like a hormone driven high school kid.

I brushed my teeth and contemplated the question of Theo's past. Was he really just a player and if so, did I care? It was true that Theo had played with me, but I hadn't been his plaything. We had played together.

129

"What exactly have you gotten yourself into Callie" I asked my reflection. It was no use, I had no idea but I knew I wasn't going to stop.

* * * *

I spent the afternoon bargain shopping. I picked up a painting of a seascape in a driftwood frame, and some mercury candlesticks. I knew I shouldn't be spending money on the apartment but I wanted it to be mine. As I hung the picture on the wall near the bed I realized I'd never set up a space of my own like this before. Sure I'd had a dorm in college and graduate housing, but from there I'd moved to Henry's. His style was so polished, so much more demanding than mine. I thought of the cold silver and black lines that dominated the home we'd shared together and realized for the first time that every purchase had been driven by his choices.

We'd pretended for years that we were in things together, but how many times had I swallowed my own opinion for the greater good.

"And I was the designer you mother trucker," I said. For the first time in a long time I was trying not to swear to be a better person, not because Henry required it.

I surveyed my increasingly homey space. Windows cracked open, the white curtains billowed in the breeze. My beachy painting made me think of trips to the beach in California as a girl, before my parents had died. Those were happy days of sunlight and sand between my toes. The seascape felt solitary and tranquil but not lonely, nothing lonely about this space at all I realized with pride.

My phone rang, and for a moment my heart leapt out of my chest hoping it was Theo until my brain remembered he didn't have my number.

"You aren't spiraling, are you?"

It was Cara.

"No, I'm nesting," I said. "I'm channeling my grief into productivity. I'm making this space my own, and it looks pretty darn good if I do say so myself."

"Fabulous. Now channel your grief into a walk with me. It's beautiful outside, I'll meet you at Greenlake in fifteen."

"Deal," I said. I grabbed my running shoes and headed out the door. As I walked past Theo's door I totally resisted the urge to knock.

∗ ∗ ∗ ∗

Greenlake Park was equidistant between my apartment and Cara's house. A large man-made lake with an amphitheater on one side and a community center on the other; the narrow path was often crowded with moms pushing baby strollers, packs of bikers, and running clubs. A 2.7 mile loop on the inside, and 3.1 mile on the outside trail it was the perfect distance for a run or a walk with a friend.

"Run or walk?" Cara asked, when she spotted me. She was stretching her calves on the curb.

"Walk, I'm tired," I said, thinking of my sleepless night.

"Deal. How was your Monday?" Cara said, snaking her arm through mine as we started walking along the winding asphalt path that framed Greenlake.

"You mean how was day five of my life without Henry?"

"You know the amount of time isn't totally relevant here. You are going to grieve and deal with this on your own timeline."

"Is that the kind of thing you tell all your patients?" We shifted to the side at the sound of a bicyclist approaching from behind.

"You are not a patient; you are my friend."

"Well, as your friend," I said. "I appreciate the free counseling and I think it was a good day. I feel like I'm coming out of my funk."

"Good." Cara squeezed my arm before letting go. We

picked up the pace, strolling arm in arm, weaving between couples and packs of moms and strollers. Greenlake became incredibly busy on warm summer nights. It felt good to be out in the world.

"So, today was day one of my Callie vacation," I said. "No work. No obligations. Just time to focus on what I want and have the courage to ask for it." A sly smile escaped me before I could pull it in. I couldn't help it, just saying the words *I want* out loud conjured up Theo's face and his touch.

"What aren't you telling me?" Cara said, stopping. Her eyes widened at my smirk. "Oh my God you did something." She swatted my arm. "It's that guy. That one you told me about."

"Maybe . . ."

We started walking again as a pack of cyclists zoomed past us.

"Spill it."

"So . . . His name is Theo. And he came over last night . . ." And I told her about the five nights and what we'd done the night before.

Cara stopped walking, jaw hanging open. "Theo says he can cure you in five days and you came like three times?"

"Four," I said. "I came four times. You really need to pay attention to the details."

"So it's like therapy, but not therapy. Sex."

"Yep," I said. "He will heal me with sex. So he says."

We started walking again. Cara leaned in as she whispered. "And you are sure he isn't some sort of pervert? You know this could be the way he lures women into his trap."

"He does not seem like a psycho, Cara, and it's not a trap it's consensual sex," I said. "And he seems thoughtful. He seems kind." We rounded the path near the outdoor stadium bleachers.

Early evening light filtered through the trees reflecting on the water. I suddenly wished that Theo was walking beside me. I wondered if he had ever seen the lake in a light this beautiful. It occurred to me that I didn't know whether or not he walked around Greenlake. I didn't know a thing about how he liked to spend his free time. The only thing I did know was that he'd found a way to make me come multiple times without taking off all my clothes and he loved to please women.

"He seems kind." Cara repeated, her skepticism clear. "You don't know this guy at all do you."

"I know it's a little crazy. And I'm not saying it's

rational, but I'm not looking for a boyfriend. It's five nights." I thought about lying beside Theo the night before, running my hand along his long lean body, my fingers tracing his scar. "He has secrets, not bad ones. He has this scar, but he won't talk about it."

"You saw a scar?"

"Well, yes, I told you we were almost naked."

"And he wouldn't talk about it?"

"Nope."

I could see the therapist wheels in her blonde head spinning. "Makes me wonder who or what he wants to forget."

"Yeah, I don't know," I said, wishing I knew more about him. We walked for a few moments in silence and I wondered if Cara was right. Was Theo trying to forget something from his past, or even more intriguing, someone? He did seem to know a lot about broken hearts.

"I don't know if I could do it," Cara said. "Not get attached. If he is as good as you say, that sounds pretty addictive. How do you not get attached to a man who can make you come you said three?"

I shook my head.

"Oh my God, four," she whispered. "I wanted to say four but even then my brain was like, no way, that's not possible. That man made you come four times. Seriously, that is going to be hard to walk away from."

"We made a deal," I said. "And I'm not a liar."

"But is he a liar?"

"He's a good guy, Cara. I can tell." I ignored that inner voice that wanted to remind me I had thought Henry was a good guy too, once upon a time.

"So, did his cock tell you that?" She said giving me a half smile.

"I told you I didn't get nearly enough of it to know." We both collapsed into a fit of giggles and I wondered if I was telling the truth. Could I make love and play with Theo for five nights and not want anything more? Or, was I just setting myself up for a different kind of disappointment and heartbreak? After all, in five nights he'd still be my neighbor. It wasn't like I could move across town, I'd just signed a one-year lease and my apartment was going to be my oasis, my sanctuary. I was not going to let some guy ruin that for me was I?

Cara stopped walking. She grabbed my arm and spun me around. "Other way. Other way." She picked up the pace. "Don't look back."

I immediately looked back.

Henry and Sophia.

His Five Night Stand

Hands swinging as they walked, a huge smile on Henry's face. He leaned in to talk with Sophia who looked up at him adoringly. They were clearly head over heels with each other.

"I don't want to see this, I don't want this to be real," I whispered, stunned. The memory of Henry and his betrayal swept over me like a cold ocean wave. I had felt so strong and here it was so fresh, the rejection. I had given him years and he had picked someone else, and not just anyone else, this girl, this pretty pixie girl with blonde hair and a yoga body that looked ridiculously bendable. I felt like an oaf by just existing. Here was Henry and the girl he had picked over me.

"Keep walking," Cara said, dragging me forward as my broken heart grew roots and anchored me into place. There was Henry with his new love and what was I doing, fucking around with some good looking guy who promised me nothing but a dead end. My vision blurred with tears.

Henry stopped walking ahead of me in the path. Our eyes met.

His face fell and he dropped Sophia's hand to give me a tentative wave.

I didn't wave back. Seeing him look at me I snapped out of my daze walking away.

"Get me out of here," I whispered walking in stride next to Cara. "I can't see him, not like this . . ."

I felt like the air had grown thin, I couldn't fill my lungs. I felt weak. With a single glance, Henry had reminded me of all my failures, all the years I'd given him, and all the nights I'd wanted him to choose me when he'd really been waiting to choose someone else. I had believed in him for so long, and I had missed so many signs. I doubted myself, my inner radar, my ability to know what was real from what I wanted to be.

And now there was Theo.

I'd just agreed to a five night stand with a man I barely knew. Was that really the right way to take care of myself? Was I doing the right thing, or making another horrible mistake?

CHAPTER 14

When I got home that night there was a notecard on the floor.

Night 2—9:00 p.m.? T

I thought about knocking on his door or writing back and telling him not to come, but I felt so sad and mixed up I did nothing until he knocked on my door that night.

I sat on my futon listening, knowing Theo was right outside. If I was going to break this off, I owed him an explanation. I had agreed to five nights but now I wasn't sure what I wanted to do. I needed to make up my mind.

The knocking continued.

I'd taken a shower after my walk. Wrapping my terry cloth robe tight around my body I answered the door.

"Hello love," Theo said, his face lighting up and then falling at my expression. "What is wrong?"

"I'm sorry, I'm a mess but I'll be all right . . ." I burst into tears and stepped away from the door embarrassed and horrified with myself. I'd cried in the shower trying to get all the emotion out but clearly I'd missed a stockpile of tears.

Theo stepped inside and closed the door softly. Then

he wrapped me into a big bear hug.

"Don't be nice to me," I sobbed. "If you're nice to me, I'll cry. It's one of my personal issues."

"I think you are already crying, love," he said. "So, nice I will be."

He rested his chin on my head and rocked me back and forth slowly. I inhaled deeply against his shirt. He wore a black button down and when I turned my head I could see pearl buttons running down the front. He smelled like eucalyptus and a musky spice this time. I wondered if it was cologne or just his scent.

"What happened to you today? Besides the fact you have been using your junior designer skills to spruce things up." His voice was soft, kind and comforting. I wanted his arms to stay wrapped around me forever, I wanted to disappear in this warm place. "You have transformed this space, love. I'm impressed."

His compliments were lost on me. I could think of nothing but Henry and my pain. "I saw him today," I hiccupped. "Walking with a friend. I saw Henry, my ex. His name is Henry . . ."

"I remember his name," he said, his voice full of a smile.

"He was with the girl he left me for and it made me

feel pathetic and horrible. I thought I was doing so well, but it made me think that I'm not over him at all and maybe I'm just a mess and maybe what we did isn't good for me . . ."

"Just breathe," he said, smoothing my hair. He took my hand and walked me to the futon. I had not pulled it down yet. I think some part of me left it set up thinking that it was a sign I hadn't decided what was going to happen that night. "Look, this thing with you and me. What we are, what we do together is about feeling good, being together. It has nothing to do with the man who broke your heart and we will only do what you want, you got it?"

"I got it," I said, nodding. I did feel better beside him. The feeling of his arms wrapping around me, the warmth of him. The way he looked at me as if I were the most beautiful woman in the world.

He sat beside me, holding my hand. His face stubbly, he had a rugged sexy look that made me want to run my fingers across his cheek. His dark hair was sprinkled with something that looked like dust. I couldn't resist and I brushed my fingers through his hair.

"You're messy," I said, managing a smile.

"It's work," he said. "Plaster. I started some new molds today."

"The gallery?"

"I'm a sculptor," he said.

I swallowed thinking of his hands on clay, marble, and stone. His fingers were long and sexy, his hands strong and large. I felt the familiar heat building between my legs. It felt good to be near him. Was it a mistake to feel good? "So, what were you sculpting today?"

"Today I was working on something kind of special," he said, smiling. He leaned over and kissed my temple. "I was thinking of a beautiful woman while I worked."

"You were." I closed my eyes and leaned into him. "What were you thinking about her?"

"I was hoping she would see me tonight, and the day felt so long as I waited to see her." He kissed my forehead softly and brushed a stray hair off my face.

I opened my eyes and turned to look at him. His blue eyes focused on me, his breathing shallow. I could feel the heat rolling off his body. "So, did you go to her?" I asked, taking his hand and placing it on my thigh under my robe.

"I knocked on her door and when she didn't answer I knocked some more."

"And did she answer?"

His hands slid up my thighs kneading my flesh with just the right pressure.

"She did and she shared her heartbreak with me, and she was beautiful and fragile and I begged her to let me love her that night."

"And what did she say?"

"Let me love you tonight, Callie," he whispered his mouth against my neck. "Let me take your heartbreak away, let's bring each other joy, I need this. If you let me I can make you feel good, if you want this, only if you say yes."

I pushed him away and looked him square in the face. His confession startled me. "You need this? It isn't just me."

"Of course not," he said. "I need this too. The way you make me feel, it heals me somehow." He brushed a lock of hair behind my ear and my whole body tingled.

"Why do you need healing?" I asked.

"Everyone is hiding from some heartbreak, love."

He's running from something or someone I thought, remembering Cara's theory about his scar. I knew nothing about this man and I wasn't even sure that this was good for my aching heart, but I no longer cared.

I took his face in my hands and kissed him, gently pushing my tongue into his mouth. Exploring him, probing him. I'd never kissed a man like that, with such control, taking what I wanted.

I stood and turned to face him and undid the tie of my robe. I dropped the tie to the ground and let my robe fall to my feet.

I stood naked before him, my hair still damp hanging around my shoulders. I didn't worry about the fact that I hadn't done my hair this time, or picked my favorite gloss. This was me, all of me. It felt completely honest, standing before him. I had been thinking I needed to be someone else with Theo but really I wanted to be myself. "I need this too."

"You are so beautiful, so perfect, exactly the way you are," he said, his blue eyes locking with mine.

We didn't bother to set up the bed. Instead Theo dragged the whole mattress onto the floor and we fell upon each other. We rolled around the make-shift bed as I stripped off his clothes unsnapping the buttons of his black shirt. Then I straddled him, wrapping my legs around his jeans, his rising cock pushing up against me.

"Are you going to make love to me tonight?" I asked breathless, my fingers pulling on his belt. I couldn't get him naked fast enough.

"But it's only day two," he said, flipping me over onto my back.

His Five Night Stand

"Oh my God you and your rules!" I found myself laughing as I pulled his belt off and undid the buttons of his jeans, sliding them off like I had the night before. He wore a pair of black tight boxers that hugged his enormous bulge. My fingers played with the waistband.

"The rules are the rules, love."

"So what happens day two?" I asked breathless and wanting him. "Please tell me we are both going to be naked tonight?"

He nodded slowly and I slid his underwear off, exposing his enormous cock. It was long and incredibly wide. I gasped thinking about it pushing inside me. I had never seen such a beautiful penis. I wanted to put it in my mouth. I wanted to feel it slide inside of me. I wanted him to fuck every part of my body.

"Night two, love. I explore you more." he said, rolling onto his side and pressing up against me, his enormous cock pushing against my side. His mouth on my neck he moved down my body over my breasts his tongue playing with my nipples as he touched my clitoris. He had touched me the night before through the fabric of my panties, but now it was his fingers, his hot skin against my throbbing wetness.

"And remind me again why we wait?" I gasped.

"We wait until we can't bear to wait any longer."

"What if I can't wait now?" I was shocked by my boldness. I was basically begging him to fuck me properly, not that I was complaining about these other games.

"Just enjoy this," he said, moving his fingers in slow circles while he sucked on my tits. I felt my breath quickening. I was shocked by how quickly he got me going. His mouth moving to my belly, he started moving down.

"Wait. Where are you going?"

"I'm going to taste you," he said, his mouth inching closer and closer.

"I don't know," I said, a nervous tightness seizing in my belly. "What if you don't like it, what if you don't enjoy . . ."

"Why wouldn't I enjoy tasting you?"

"It makes me nervous," I said, my body tightening as my self-consciousness beat out my desire. I felt like my mind had just pulled the breaks on my out of control body.

"Then breathe deeply and feel this," He said, placing my hand on his cock. "You wonder if I like what I'm doing, just feel this."

Then his mouth was on me again, I could feel his hardness pressing against me as he moved down my body nibbling and sucking. Then his hands were on my pussy spreading my lips wide, and his mouth was between my legs.

I gasped as a wave of pleasure moved through me. My head rolled back, mouth open, eyes closed. I felt him against me, his lips sucking on me, and his tongue probing me. I had never felt anything so intimate and so hot. Henry had gone down on me before, but I had always felt like it was hurried, obligatory, and very infrequent. Theo moved against me as if my pussy was the most delicious and sexy thing he'd ever tasted. He touched me as if he couldn't control himself.

His tongue moved in circles against my clitoris the pressure increasing. His breathing steady, I could feel his cock against my leg, hard and throbbing. At times my mind would object with some worry. Did I taste good? Was I all right? And then I'd feel him moving with a frenzy, as if he couldn't control himself. I felt a quickening deep in my core as he massaged me with his mouth and then I felt his fingers against me. He spread me wider pushing a single finger inside me, back and forth, in and out. He fucked me with his mouth and his fingers. Then I felt another finger slide into place, he moved slowly and he paused, his voice breathless. "This okay, love?" he asked.

"Yes, yes please, yes," I said, eyes closed as he spread me wider sliding in and out, his mouth on my pussy, fingers fucking me deeper, harder. His fingers pressing against the sensitive spot right near my opening. I had never really been a big believer in a G spot, but I was pretty sure he had found it.

Then a third finger, I felt a fullness as he moved back and forth, faster, faster, he timed the thrusting with his mouth and I forgot that this was his mouth and finger, I imagined his enormous cock spreading me apart, I thought about my thighs opening up and the sides of my pussy expanding and dripping wet. I wanted him inside me. I wanted him deeper. I wanted more.

"Don't stop, don't stop, don't stop," I whispered the words coming out of me uncensored. "More baby, more, harder."

He followed my instructions.

"Deeper."

"Faster."

And I wasn't even aware of my body or the mechanics of what we were doing, I was only sexual energy and pleasure as waves of an orgasm rocked through me. I screamed, back arching as my body shook while he held me in place still sucking on me, his fingers still probing, the orgasm rocked on and on until he lifted his mouth and kissed me softly between the legs. The feeling of his lips made me shiver.

"Oh, my God," I said, suddenly self-conscious again.

"You. Taste." He moved up my body softly kissing me stopping on my breasts to suck. "You taste like sex." Then he kissed me opening my mouth with his tongue and I tasted the salty spice of myself. It tasted raw and sexy and it made me want to fuck.

"I get your five nights," I said, kissing his neck, my hands searching for his cock. "You tease me until I beg you to fuck me. Is that how this goes? What if I beg you now, what if I can't stand it?"

He inhaled and rolled over onto his back when my hands found his cock. I moved up and down the shaft feeling the heat of him. "It's not about that, love," He said, his eyes closed. "This is about pleasure."

"Taking it slow?" I laughed, and buried my face in his neck while I rubbed his cock up and down, faster and faster.

"This takes self-control," he said. "Do you know how hard it is not to flip you over and take you right now?" He turned to his side, his blue eyes locking on mine.

"Why don't you?"

"Because I want to explore every inch of you. I want

you to remember that you are magnificent that you can come a thousand ways without my cock."

"And with it?"

"Oh, you'll come love," he said. He moved my hand away from his hardness. "And then I will too."

"Not until then?"

"You are jumping ahead," he said. His fingers moving back to my pussy in slow circles. "Now let's see what happens if we do this . . ."

His mouth on my nipple he sucked as he explored me with his fingers, this time right before I came, he slid his fingers inside me again his fingers hooking and pressing up against that sensitive spot, I could feel my pussy pulsing all around him, a heartbeat between my legs.

After I came again, he pulled me against his body and rested his head against me. "Can I ask you something?" I asked.

"Sure . . ." He sounded cautious.

"Why do you do this?"

"Do what?"

"Sleep with women, five nights only. Don't you wonder what would happen if you stayed. I mean I'm not pressuring you but surely if five nights are good, wouldn't six, or seven . . ."

"I've been with women longer," he said.

"And?"

"I'm not made for commitment," he said. "I tried it once. I can't do it again. This keeps things simple."

"Well, I know you're good at it," I said, feeling a heat again at the weight of his body beside me. I wanted to feel him underneath me, to ride his cock and slide up and down on it, I wanted so much more.

"Did she break your heart?" I asked cautiously.

"In a manner of speaking."

"What does that mean?"

"She died," he said.

"I'm sorry."

"Don't be, you didn't do it."

"Well, I can still be sorry."

I could feel him pulling away from me, he rolled ever so slightly away and I felt as though I'd pushed too hard. "I'm sorry," I said. "I struggle with the unknown so I ask questions, and these five nights with you, it's pushing me in ways I've never experienced."

"You seem experienced to me," he said, his eyes lighting up again.

"Can I ask you something else?" I said. "I know you said it's not until night five, but tonight, can I make you

151

feel good, will you let me?"

His eyes sparkled. "There is one way."

He rolled me over onto my back and straddled my belly. His fingers between my legs he opened me up, bending down to lick and nibble. I whimpered and moaned as he pressed against me harder, the sensation of his throbbing cock resting against my belly. Then he slid back and straddled my face, his cock and balls above me. I took the tip of his penis with my fingertips massaging the drop of cum at the top away. "You are so hard," I gasped as he worked on my pussy, moving faster and faster.

I took him into my mouth the tip of his cock so large, I sucked back and forth wanting to make him wet, wanting him to think of fucking me as I slid him in and out while his tongue played with my clitoris. We got into a rhythm. I rocked my head back trying to get more of him into my mouth pushing deeper, harder, sucking more, faster, faster.

We moved together rocking back and forth, his lips sucking on my clitoris, his tongue pushing into me, my mouth opening up wider, wetter, I almost choked on his girth. Back and forth, in and out, I sucked harder faster until I felt his breath change a moan escaping his lips. Then his mouth on me, I arched my back pressing against him screaming and moaning as waves of an orgasm shook my body. His cock shuddering, he came all over my breasts until he collapsed against me shuddering.

We slept. We awoke late into the night, or early in the morning depending on your point of view. It was 5:00 a.m.

Theo leaned over and whispered in my ear. "I have to go, love," he said. "Night two, you made me fall asleep in your arms. You are a rule breaker."

"I don't remember that rule," I said, wrapping my arms around his neck. "Don't go, not yet."

"I have to work soon. I have to shower."

I took his hand and placed it between my legs. "Shower with me." I said, shocking myself. "Please, don't leave."

I heard him moan softly and he rolled on top of me, his mouth on mine, cock hardening as we kissed.

"Please," I said between kisses.

"You are very persuasive," he said, smiling as he stood and offered me his hand.

In the shower, the warm water poured over our bodies. We stood beneath the spray letting the water cover us, our bodies pressed together. His mouth against mine, he kissed me softly, sweetly even as he ran his fingers across my tits and down to my pussy. "You are going to make me late," he said, grinning. Then dropping to his knees in front of me. He pulled the lips of my pussy apart, supporting my back with his hand, he scooted me towards the tiles. They felt cold against my back but I didn't care. He used them as leverage to press against me harder and faster, his mouth fucking me as my legs grew weak. He reached up and pinched my tits with his finger tips and I came screaming as his tongue pushed inside me.

He held me shuddering and shaking against him. "I will remember the taste of you all day," he said, kissing me.

I dropped to my knees. "And now you. I need this, I need to feel you." I said, taking his cock with my hand, the other cradling his balls. He moaned and closed his eyes leaning against the wall, I turned and knelt before him so I could take him into my mouth the water covering us, warm and slick. I sucked on him harder and harder this time I was able to open my mouth wider, taking him deep into my throat. I relaxed and managed not to gag as I pulled him in deeper and deeper.

"Oh love, you are good, so good," he said, his hand on my head he pushed into me, not too hard, just enough for me to know that he was close, then I felt him coming into my mouth with a shuddering and a shaking. I spit out into the water, letting it rinse through my mouth. He lifted me up by the hand and pulled me against him.

"That is against the rules," he said, smiling and kissing my ear.

"What else is against the rules," I said.

"Getting attached," he kissed me fiercely this time lifting me up so I could straddle him. I felt the tip of his cock pressing against my throbbing pussy and could feel him thinking, considering as he moved me up and down, playing with how close we were. He was strong and it would take just a single tilt.

Water pouring over me, my pussy dripping, I ached for him. I felt the tip of his cock flirting with my pussy, my lips opening for him. I wanted him so badly but I knew this was recklessness. I was on the pill, but the pill wasn't 100 percent and we had pieces of paper guaranteeing we were disease free, but we still barely knew each other. In that moment my want was stronger than my brain. I didn't care and pushed myself against his tip, I could feel him begin to enter me. I moaned at the sensation of spreading open. And then he stopped.

"Not yet," he whispered, setting me softly on the ground. "Not yet, love, but soon."

I thought I might collapse from desire and disappointment.

He kissed me good bye before he left. I crawled back

into bed aching for a man I still barely knew. Who was I?

CHAPTER 15

I found another note under my door the next evening. I leaned against the door as I read.

Callie—Night 3 will need to wait. You are addictive and I'm afraid of moving too fast with you. Rest and know I crave your touch. If you will have me again, I'll see you tomorrow night—T

My knees felt weak. T.

I tried not to feel disappointed. I could wait another night, couldn't I? I tried not to read more into his words. He craved my touch, he feared moving too fast. This was part of his five-day routine, I couldn't allow myself to want or hope for more.

The card stock felt solid and strong in my hands making me think of his arms around my waist and his mouth against mine and other parts of my body. When we were together, the things Theo did to me, the way he touched me caused me no shame, only pleasure.

I remembered with sweetness the way he'd soothed away my tears. Seeing Henry had rattled me the arrogant bastard. What right did he have to walk around my lake with his new girlfriend? As stupid as that sounded I did feel as though he'd invaded some unspoken territorial agreement. You stay downtown with your expensive car and fancy restaurants and leave me with my bohemian coffee shops, corner cafes, and sunlight filled parks. Henry had hurt me, and the shock of seeing him reminded me that the wound was fresh, but in the morning light after two nights of loving from Theo, I felt a little stronger, more sure of myself.

The man I thought I loved didn't want me, so what. I was a desirable and lovable woman who was just beginning to understand the things her body could do. I had never felt this way physically about Henry. The pain of losing him was still present, but the curiosity I felt for Theo and myself felt like it might just be tipping the scales in my favor.

And what about the woman who had broken Theo's heart? This mystery woman had died. She was a ghost, a memory that I couldn't compete with. I closed my eyes and held the note to my chest feeling dizzy with emotion. "Idiot," I whispered out loud. "It's five nights, nothing more. It doesn't matter if he loves a ghost or a hundred women before or after you. All you have is now."

I took a breath and stood tall. My neurotic inner war would need to continue later. Sure I was having the most amazing sex of my life with an almost total stranger, but if

His Five Night Stand

I wanted to have clean clothes the next time my tall dark and handsome showed up, I needed to do laundry.

I scrounged up some quarters and grabbed a basket full of dirty clothes.

The laundry room was in the basement down three flights of stairs at the end of the hall from Billie's office. The sound of laughter in the laundry room echoed down the hall. I stopped walking wondering if I could slip back upstairs unnoticed. I wasn't in the mood to chat with anyone considering the last time I'd seen any of the women in this building I'd been drunk and wobbling on Theo's arm.

I had just decided to turn around when I heard footsteps behind me.

"Hey Callie, there's room for another, come on in." Shea stood in the hallway swinging an empty laundry bottle. She wore casual sweats, her pale hair in a messy topknot.

"I can come back," I said, taking a step back. "If the machines are all busy."

"Don't be dumb, it's just me and Odessa and a bottle of red wine. It's laundry night."

Odessa. I took another step back.

Theo's former lover.

Odessa knew about Theo's five nights.

Odessa knew my secrets.

At the word wine Odessa stuck her head out into the hallway spotting me.

Her black hair hung loose around her face and for once she didn't have her cats eye make up on. She looked natural and luminous wearing a tank top and jean shorts. I was instantly jealous. She had a history with Theo. I wanted to run and hide from her and my emotions. I knew I had no right to feel jealous about their past. We were not an item. We were an experiment. An idea.

"Hey there!" Odessa said, darting into the hallway and grabbing my hand. "You are not escaping. You need to come in here and join us. I want to know everything."

My heart hammered in my chest as I followed her inside, my laundry basket hooked under my arm. "Everything?"

"Let me help," Odessa said, taking my basket and setting it on a long table. She opened a machine and started sorting through my clothing separating whites and colors.

"I can do that," I said.

Shea returned with a fresh bottle of detergent. "Don't bother, she is meticulous and impossible, it's best to let Odessa do what she wants." Shea took a seat on one of the vibrating washers and gave a wicked grin. "This thing is fun, I really should kick you girls out of here and get Troy in here. I have a feeling that we could have some fun on this machine."

"Oh please," Odessa said. "You can't tell me that you and Troy haven't already done it in the laundry room." She looked at me conspiratorially. "I know for a fact they have made a game out of having sex in every room in this building."

"Not every room," Shea said, rolling her eyes.

"You fucked in Callie's room two days before she rented it," Odessa said, taking a pile of my whites and putting them in a washer.

"Guilty as charged," Shea giggled holding her hands up in surrender.

"I heard every moan," Odessa explained. "You may have noticed the walls are kind of thin."

"I hadn't really noticed," I said, cheeks burning.

"Oh please," Shea said. "It's a rite of passage to listen to Odessa moan. I remember living upstairs from you when you were in Callie's studio. This was right after I moved to Seattle. I grew up working the apple orchards of Eastern Washington. I was a walking cliché. Small town girl lost in the big city and then I heard it." Shea gripped the edge of the machine and moaned. "Oh, baby, yes, yes, yes." She rocked back and forth banging on the machine her face rapt with pleasure as she pretended to orgasm. "I was inspired to tell you the truth. Were you with Theo then or was that before?"

Something flashed in Odessa's eyes at the mention of before Theo.

"Never mind," Shea said, looking apologetic. "It doesn't matter really."

My mind was still stuck on Theo. The mention of his name made me feel a little dizzy and jealous, so inappropriately jealous. Odessa was one of the women Theo had loved before. It was a little too much for me to bear.

"A woman has a right to moan. If we aren't moaning, we need a new lover, the right lover. We deserve pleasure. And when you find the man that makes you feel every part of your body, we should hold on tight." Odessa arched one of her thinly plucked eyebrows. Was this her way of telling me that she'd heard my recent cries? My face burned even hotter and I wished I'd just stayed upstairs with my dirty clothes. I did not know how to talk to these women who were so open about sexuality, they were so raw and uncensored, I felt repressed and awkward around them.

His Five Night Stand

I took a seat on the wooden bench across from the machines. Shea poured me a red solo cup full of red wine. I knew enough about wine to know it was expensive. I imagined it was Odessa's from the pile of laundry she'd started folding, the labels and fabric told me she had money. I wondered again why she was living in The Holiday. It was a nice building, but it wasn't luxurious, it had character. I knew why I was here. I wondered what the other women's stories were.

"So," Odessa said. "I've waited long enough to ask. How are things going with . . . Theo?" She took a swig of her wine and grinned at me.

And boom. There it was.

I swallowed feeling totally exposed but slightly relieved to have the question out in the open. I didn't need to pretend it hadn't happened. I could hear the sound of her lovemaking; clearly she had heard me with Theo. Then another thought occurred to me. Maybe I could learn more about Theo without breaking his rules.

"Things, are going," I paused, unable to contain my smile. I took another big swig of wine the feeling of warmth moving through my body.

"Oh my God, did you hook her up with Theo?" Shea said, pouring me another drink. "You didn't tell me that."

Odessa shrugged. "I thought Theo and Callie might be good for each other, and I like seeing other people happy."

"And remembering you deserve happiness yourself," Shea said, lips pursing as she almost glared at her friend.

"I'm happy enough," Odessa said. "This isn't about me. It's about Callie and Theo."

"Is he still doing his five night only thing?" Shea asked me.

"Yes," I said, feeling embarrassed that his five night stand was somehow common knowledge. "We've had two nights so far."

"Two already?" Odessa said, eyebrows arching. "Interesting."

"Interesting?" I repeated.

"Nothing. It's just Theo generally likes to take things very slow. He savors his women, he worships us."

Us. I hated that. Me. I wanted to say. He worships me. I was officially losing my shit and the wine was not helping.

"Well, he told me that he would see me tomorrow, he needed a break," I said, trying not to sound too disappointed.

"Interesting," Odessa said. Again, the word with no explanation.

"Because?" I asked, craving information.

"He has a pattern and you seem to be breaking it," Odessa said, smiling. "I noticed last night he came in and went directly to work. Did he sleep with you?"

"You mean like close his eyes?"

"Yes, sleep. Theo doesn't sleep with women, he loves them and he leaves."

"He did fall asleep . . . after."

"I think you have him unsettled," Odessa said, grinning. "That is definitely not his pattern."

"I don't want to unsettle him; I mean it's just a physical thing. I understand the rules. Five nights, no getting attached."

"How could you not get attached to that cock?" Shea said, sighing. "I've heard it's gorgeous. If I wasn't madly in love with Troy, I would so want a night with Theo Manhattan."

"Manhattan?" I said. So, he had a last name. I felt like such an idiot. I didn't know it and yet it sounded familiar.

"Yes, you know the Manhattan gallery downtown?" Shea said. "You may have seen it a couple blocks down from the art museum. Theo is a sculptor and a curator. His pieces are outrageously expensive and he owns the gallery as well. He's quite the collector. Be careful." She wagged her finger back and forth playfully.

"Well, I don't think he's going to collect me," I said, getting her meaning. "Five nights, it was clear and I am just getting over someone. The last thing I need is complication."

"Oh please," Odessa said, pouring me more wine. Somehow my cup was empty again. A load of laundry washed and in the dryer now, my darks were next. Where did the time go here? "The only thing you need is complication. Women make a mistake with heartbreak. There is this thing, don't make out with anyone, don't fuck anyone. Mourn. Grieve. Bullshit, I say. When your heart is broken, take it and gift it to someone else. Be vulnerable. Be beautiful. Be strong. Let your body remind you of your power. Embrace yourself."

"She really should write self-help," Shea said, nodding with seriousness.

"When your heart breaks you feel unlovable. If you have the right frame of mind, being loved by someone else can remind you to fall in love with yourself again." Odessa had moved towards me, brushing a strand of hair off my face. "Do you feel more beautiful, Callie?"

"Yes," I whispered.

"The thing is, you never stopped being beautiful, you

just forgot."

"Kiss her!" Shea shouted snorting and laughing.

"She's not my type," Odessa said, winking. "But honey I'm not rejecting you, you are gorgeous. And I think you are getting to Theo."

"Why would I get to him?"

"Theo had his heart broken. He's more vulnerable than he wants you to believe."

"The woman he loved died," I said, my heart racing. "He told me about her, a little bit."

"He told you about Grace?"

Her name was Grace. "Not all the details." Which was not a lie.

"I saw them only once when they were together, they were extraordinary. Both beautiful. A fiery love. I could see it even then."

"I see," I said, wondering now if I really wanted to know the details.

"There was a car accident. Theo was driving."

"His scar," I whispered.

"So, you've seen it," she said.

"Um, where is this scar exactly, can you describe please?" Shea said, leaning forward red solo cup in hand.

"After Grace, Theo collapsed. That is when we really

found each other. He had stopped sculpting. He had a studio at Elliot Bay Marina but he was producing nothing. He was a wreck. I found him there one night. I had just gone through some pretty rough shit and we helped each other."

"You were lovers," I said.

"We tried to be lovers, there is a difference," she said, squeezing my hand. "We tried and in trying we helped heal each other. Theo needed healing and so did I. Then we parted ways. He's a friend, one of my best friends."

"Will he ever be over her?" I asked.

"Oh honey," Odessa smiled. "Day two and you are already wondering? Be careful with that heart of yours. You are with Theo to learn to love yourself again not fall in love . . . remember that."

"I am. I do. I'm just curious."

"When Grace died, so did a part of Theo. I think for a long time he wished he'd died on the Aurora Bridge alongside her."

"It's so sad," I whispered.

"I sent Theo your way because I saw a spark in you, a light and it reminded me of Grace a bit. I thought you two could help each other. I don't want to be the cause of more heartbreak. He's a five night man until he decides differently. Remember that."

"I remember," I said.

"Can you tell me again about where exactly that scar is?" Shea said a little too loudly. "I mean is it right here?" She pointed to her belly. "Or here, lower." She pointed between her legs.

We all burst into a fit of giggles and suddenly I felt as though I belonged.

* * * *

Drunk and with a basket full of clean clothes. I put my things away and thought about Odessa's warning. Theo had been hurt. He was a five night man. Then why did I feel something deeper? Was that all wishful thinking on my part? I felt foolish and hopeful wanting to believe that there was something more happening between us. My heart was healing. Could meaningless sex really be the cure? But maybe meaningless was the wrong word. Sex without strings? Was that a better way to think of it? My mind rebelled against this idea. It had to be more.

At least I had three more nights to decide.

Three more nights.

I decided to not worry whether or not it was love. I closed my eyes and slept.

* * * *

I dreamt again of running down the hallway in the darkness. I was searching for someone, aching for him. A familiar hand reached for me, his fingers interlacing with mine, his body warm, I knew his scent. He pulled me toward him and this time when I looked up he was no longer faceless. Theo stood above me, pulled me closer. "You're trouble," he whispered his hands sliding under my clothes, his fingers expertly working their way into my panties.

"I want you," I said. "I want you now."

He lifted me up and pressed me against the wall, my legs wrapped around his body, I could feel his cock pressing up against my wetness.

I moaned as he played with me, moving me up and down, not penetrating me, making me dizzy with lust. He played with me like he had in the shower and I felt the familiar tingling and rippling building in my core.

"Moan for me, baby," Theo whispered as my body shook and shivered with pleasure.

I awoke to the sound of Odessa next door climaxing. We both moaned and shook and for the first time I wasn't ashamed.

CHAPTER 16

There was another note under my door in the morning. *10:00 p.m. Wear something sexy.* T

I felt a quickening in my belly just looking at his handwriting on the card. Tonight, he would come to me tonight.

Wear something sexy?

What did that mean? Did he mean lingerie? Did he mean a t-shirt and yoga pants like casual sexy? Then I thought of the dress I'd worn the first night we'd really met. He'd seen me in the dress but we hadn't enjoyed each other.

That night, with some hesitation I slipped the red clingy number on with the same pair of silver heels. I pulled my hair back into a loose bun and decided to go with no panties.

At 10:00 p.m. he knocked.

I opened the door.

Theo stood there wearing a black button down, suit jacket, no tie. His hair damp, he'd slicked it back slightly so it didn't fall across his forehead. He always looked hot but seeing him in a suit I wanted to drag him into my apartment and rip off his clothes.

He shook his head when he looked at me and for a moment I wondered if I'd misread his invitation.

"You said, sexy, right?" I said, taking a step back.

"No . . . I mean, yes," He said, stepping inside. "You look perfect. So perfect." He held my face with both his hands and kissed me slowly, his tongue parting my lips and dancing over my teeth.

I moaned and pulled him closer as his tongue continued to explore me. "I missed you," I said, immediately regretting it. It sounded so relationship-ish. "I mean this is nice," I said, between kisses. "A girl could get used to this."

"You should be used to this," he said, his mouth traveling down my neck, kissing my collar bone. "You should be worshipped."

I tensed at the word. Odessa had said he worshipped women. Women. Plural. Not just me. "Is that what you like to do?" I asked, pulling away. I needed to be okay with this. I was the woman he was with right now; I was one of many. Still I was curious. "You worship us. Is that why you give women these nights?"

"I give women these nights because of what I get in return," he said. "I learn from every woman I love."

His Five Night Stand

"Every one of us," I said, giving him a wicked smile. "And you are learning from me?"

"Of course." He pulled me close and buried his face in my hair inhaling. "Would it help if I told you I couldn't stop thinking about you yesterday. I made myself stay away because needing you felt so dangerous, so hot. I wanted to be away from you for this moment."

"You needed me." My pulse sky-rocketed. Need. The word was so seductive, so intense.

"And I thought we could do something different tonight," he said.

I felt a heat flash in my core. "What did you have in mind?"

"How about cocktails out in the world?"

"You want to go out with me? Like out in the world to a bar?"

He laughed. "The night doesn't have to be only in this room Callie," he said. "Let's go have some fun."

* * * *

Theo drove a black convertible mustang. A '65 1/2. I recognized the cut of the bumper. I'd had a red mustang in high school, a '66 and I could tell from the way the engine purred that this was a V8 and had some money poured into it. He kept it parked in one of the private garages off the back alley.

The black vinyl felt cold against my back when I sat next to him. Before he started the engine he leaned over and kissed me pressing me back against the seat of the car, his hands sliding up my skirt.

He hit my no underwear zone and leaned back his eyes wide. "Aren't you a little devil?" he said.

"I love how you want me," I whispered, taking his hand and sliding it back up my skirt.

"You want this baby?" He asked his fingers moving in slow circles against my pussy. I moaned and rocked back. He had opened the garage door so a cool blue light filled the car. He kissed me, his tongue pushing deep into my mouth while he rubbed against me with his thumb, his other fingers sliding inside of me, Back and forth. He rocked against me faster and faster, the climax coming so quickly it took me by surprise. I came shaking as he kissed me hard his fingers still inside me.

"Do you know how hot you look when you are coming?"

"No," I laughed. "I've never watched."

"Well, we're going to change that." He kissed me again and backed out of the drive.

＊ ＊ ＊ ＊

174

His Five Night Stand

The bar was called The Cloud Room. The top floor of a hotel downtown, in the elevator the stop was illuminated by a bright blue cloud instead of a number. The Cloud Room had a piano bar and cozy dark tables lit by blue candles. When we walked in the hostess, a gorgeous Indian woman, greeted us her face lighting up when she saw Theo.

"Darling, it's been too long," she said, leaning in to kiss both sides of his cheek.

"Hello Lakshmi," he said, kissing her back. His kiss lingered a little longer than I liked on one cheek. "Darling."

"Your usual table," she said, smiling at me.

"Yes, please." He took my hand and I took comfort in the way he held me close. Surely he was sending this woman a message, I was with him. This meant something if only for tonight.

The dark booth was in the corner facing the piano bar and French doors that led outside.

A grey haired gentleman wearing a black suit and a beret played piano, a large glass bowl full of dollar bills in front of him. It wasn't crowded. After all it was a weeknight, but from glancing around the room, I felt certain this was a place for regulars. Theo was a regular, that's all, I told myself, even after I caught several women giving him familiar smiles.

"So, do you know her?" I asked, taking a sip of a martini. "The hostess."

His eyebrow arched. "Yes, I know her."

"Oh."

"Do you want to know how I know her? Do I know her biblically?"

"It doesn't matter, it's none of my business."

"We saw each other briefly," he said. "And yes, I've seen her naked."

"That's cool."

"You don't need to be happy about it, but I'm not going to lie to you."

"You won't?"

"Never," he said. He slid closer to me in the booth. "Callie, you are different from other women I've been with. I can feel you struggling with our agreement, but I can also tell that you want this. I find your emotions compelling; you are so beautiful to me even as you question everything."

"So, the fact that I'm neurotic and freaked out about all of this half of the time is a plus," I said. "To be honest, one moment I'm good with it, the next I'm confused. I'm trying, I'm really trying here."

"Everything about you is a plus. You aren't afraid to

be vulnerable. I like that."

I leaned against him and held his hand, resting our entwined fingertips on his leg. "I know I may seem overwhelmed," I whispered, lifting our hands and placing them closer to his crotch. I could feel his pants swell and I slipped my hand out of his moving for his zipper. "But you make me want to try things," I murmured. "And I'm okay if this is all we are, this feeling, this passion. I want to know that part of myself. I want you to help me find those pieces inside of me."

I grasped his shaft with my hand and moved slowly up and down, circling the tip slowly, rubbing my finger across the top of him. I ached imagining what it would feel like to slide him between my legs. Theo's breathing changed, his body tensed up as I stroked him.

"You make me want to be naughty," I whispered my mouth against his ear. I had never spoken to a man like that. It was exhilarating.

His eyes closed. He leaned his head back inhaling and exhaling slowly. "You are dangerous," he said, opening his eyes and placing his hand on mine. "Let's finish what you started, come outside with me."

As the music played, he slipped himself back inside his pants and took my hand leading me through the maze of tables to the back doors. We walked out the French doors into the night air, stars glittering overhead. There was a chill in the air. Theo took off his coat and draped it over my shoulders.

We stood on a small patio in the middle of a sprawling rooftop garden.

"Here love," he said, leading me towards a dark corner of the patio. We stood beside a stone wall covered with ivy, a series of clear oversized orbs hung back and forth between the wall and a trellis forming a ceiling of glittering lights. I held his hand and looked at the lights and then higher into the star filled sky.

"It's beautiful here," I said, "In the middle of the city, I never knew this place existed."

"And I never knew of you," he said, spinning me around his lips on mine, he kissed me, his tongue moving with authority. His hands grasping my back with a strength I hadn't felt before. He pressed against me leaning me into the cool ivy of the wall. I felt his cock grow hard as we kissed.

"I want you," I said, breathless and aching for him. "I want this." I pressed my hand up against his hardness while I slipped my tongue in his mouth. I felt high on control. I wanted to own his body.

His Five Night Stand

"I've been waiting for you to ask for what you want," he said, his eyes closed, head rocking back.

"I have been asking, I've been begging."

"It's different now," he said, brushing a strand of hair off my forehead. "The way you talk to me; the way you move with me. I can tell what you really want. I can feel your need. It's irresistible."

"Make love to me then," I said, moving closer to him. I whispered in his ear, licked his throat tasting the salt of him. "Make love to me. Fuck me. Turn me inside out. Call it whatever you want as long as this night ends with your cock inside me. I can't wait any longer. I can't. You mustn't make me wait another night." As the words poured out of me at a breathless rate, I felt the wetness between my legs. I took his hand and guided it up under the hem of my skirt. I gasped as he slid two of his fingers inside of me. He moaned and lowered his head against mine.

"You feel what you do to me?" I whispered, rocking my body slightly so I could feel his fingers moving up and down. This time I moved against his fingers, I took what I wanted sliding up and down, deeper, harder. "You make me wet with the sound of your voice."

"It's so hard to say no to you," he said, as his fingers slid in and out of me. I felt him stretch his thumb up against

179

the nub of my clitoris. He rolled across it with every thrust.

I moaned and rocked my head back. "Don't say no," I whispered.

We were standing so close together. He was fucking me with his fingers, our faces inches from each other our voices breathless and full of wanting.

"It's night three," he said. "It's too soon."

I pushed him deeper and moaned leaning into him. "Please," I whispered. "I need you. I need this. I need this now." And the building ripple of pleasure rocked through my body and I felt my body shivering and quivering around his fingers.

"Did you feel that?" I whispered kissing his cheek, his lips, pressing against him. He nodded and moaned softly.

"I want more of you; I want all of you. Tonight. Please."

He slid his fingers out of me and pushed them between my lips. I could taste myself, and I wasn't ashamed or embarrassed. He pulled me close, kissing me with an intensity that made me gasp.

Then he pulled back and leaned his forehead against mine. He exhaled as if trying to catch his breath after a run. "I need a minute," he said, laughing. Then he looked at me and smiled. "You are worth changing plans for Callie."

"What do you mean?"

"Stay with me tonight," he said, interlacing his fingers with mine. "I'd get us a room, but I want you in my bed tonight. Will you come home with me, lover?"

"Yes," I blurted, throwing my arms around his neck covering his face with kisses, his lips, his chin, his throat. "Take me home. Take me home now."

He kissed my cheek and held my hand, swinging it as we walked through the moonlit garden back into the club. We drained our drinks and he left a stack of bills on the table. In the elevator, we made out as we dropped floor by floor. Pressed against the mirrored wall, I opened my eyes so I could see us kissing.

"We're beautiful," I whispered and leaned in to kiss him again as the doors opened into the lobby. "We're beautiful and I don't want to stop."

I heard the sound of a throat clearing and turned to see an elderly couple standing arm in arm waiting for the elevator.

"Excuse us," I said, giggling and dragging Theo by the hand. I had never made out with someone in public like this and been caught, I had never felt so care free before, so unconcerned with being judged and measured.

I heard the old woman's voice calling after us as we

walked through the revolving door. "Don't worry dear, I remember those days well."

CHAPTER 17

We returned to The Holiday. As we walked hand in hand to the back door off of the alley, I realized how my mood had suddenly shifted from pure lust to a nervous energy. We were going to have sex. Of course we'd had different forms of sex for a couple of nights, but this was different. I was going to make love with Theo Manhattan.

"After you," he said, a shy smile crossing his face as he held the door open for me.

We walked up the three flights of stairs, my pulse racing from the climb and anticipation of his hands and other parts on and in my body. "So, you're going to show me your room," I said, calling back over my shoulder. "That's very personal."

"You're the first woman I've shown it to since moving in," he said.

"Yeah right," I laughed, certain he was full of shit. And did it really matter anyway? I had agreed to this game. Five nights and nothing more. I gave him my commitment to not commit and he promised to heal my broken heart. There was a freedom here I had never experienced. It was only night three and I already felt healed.

Of course my recent breakdown over Henry suggested I had some healing left to do, but I felt my shattered core turning a corner, the broken pieces fusing together by passion and love from this man. I could have this satisfaction without commitment, pleasure for pleasure alone. I had spent years always thinking about the next step of a relationship, the implications of a kiss or a second or third date. So much time trying to figure something out instead of just letting myself enjoy the person beside me.

Theo took out his key ring, unlocking the series of locks on the door.

"So, what's with all the extra security anyway," I said. "You worried about the neighborhood?"

He shrugged and held the door open as I stepped inside. "Just making sure that only the right people have passage, love."

The lights were off.

"Is Odessa home or is she . . .?" I asked, my voice trailing off. I hoped we were alone, I wanted to be alone.

"She's out tonight," he said. "She won't be home until morning. She was rather mysterious about it actually."

Alone.

Theo flipped on the hall light and the enormous chandelier I remembered from the party. The living room still looked exotic and overly decorated for a University apartment but it looked more lived in and personal this time. There were magazines on a coffee table beside a half full cup of coffee.

"This way," Theo whispered leading me across the room to what I assumed was his bedroom. He took out a key and unlocked the door.

"Your room is locked as well?" I asked my stomach flip flopping with nerves.

"Odessa and I respect each other's privacy."

The room was completely white. White walls, white bedding, long white curtains and shades, a thick shag carpet covered most of the dark hardwood floor. The walls were bare except for an enormous floor to ceiling mirror that covered the wall facing the bed. The mirror had an ornate wood frame, carvings of cherubs and apples and berries dangled from the edges. It took up the whole wall.

It was a gorgeous piece of furniture reflecting the only other object in the room, the bed I desperately wanted to fall into with this man.

"The room was built around the mirror," Theo whispered, wrapping his arms around me from behind. We faced the mirror his dark hair falling over his face as he kissed my neck. "The Holiday was a dance studio at one point," he said. "Back in the '20s. They converted the building and left some pieces. There used to be more mirrors. This is the only one that hasn't been broken." As he stood behind me, his body pressed against mine, I felt the heat building between my legs. He kissed me softly, his hands in my hair; he unpinned the loose bun at the top of my head. My hair unfurled spilling over my shoulders.

"You've come undone," he whispered. There were kisses on my neck with every breath.

I was unable to tear my gaze away from our reflection in the mirror. Eyes wide open I stood in my red dress, my hair loose around my shoulders. Theo in black behind me, his arms wrapped around my body, hands moving up and down; he would start at my waist and then slide up over my left breast, his fingers playing with the neckline of my dress.

"I want to take you slowly," he whispered.

"Please don't," I said, turning I pressed my mouth against his, my hands fumbling with his belt. He responded instantly, I felt him harden as I unzipped his pants, his mouth never leaving mine as we stumbled backwards towards the bed, his hands on my dress inching it up over my hips.

He threw me down on the bed, my dress half up.

His Five Night Stand

"Tell me what you want," he said, his eyes locking on mine.

"I want your mouth on me," I said. "I want you to taste me. I want your fingers in my pussy. I want you to make me moan."

The words poured out of me without embarrassment, without judgment. I wanted what I wanted, and I would no longer be ashamed to ask for what I needed.

He gave me a half-smile and his breathing deepened as he dropped to his knees, his face between my legs. He parted my lips with his fingertips, his mouth pressing against my clit sucking and kissing. I cried out as a wave of pleasure rolled through me, my hands sliding over my breasts. I pinched my nipples as his tongue pressed against me.

"I love how you taste," he said, licking me and nibbling as he inched my dress up with one hand. "You taste like sex. You make me want to fuck."

I moaned feeling the energy building between my legs. "More, more . . . I need more . . ."

"Wait love" he said, the kisses between my legs softening. "Open your eyes."

I hadn't even realized I'd closed them. I opened and watched as he stood and unbuttoned his shirt, dropping it to the floor. He slid off his black dress pants and stood before me in his boxers. He moved to take them off as well.

"No, let me," I said, sitting up. I scooted towards him, my legs wrapping around him, my face against his chest. I licked and kissed him running my fingers down the line from his belly button. I slid his black boxers off revealing his enormous hard cock. I pushed him forward and dropped to my knees in front of him holding his hardness between my fingers. He throbbed, his skin hot, a drop of cum rising to the surface as I ran my fingers up and down. "This is mine tonight," I said. Leaning forward, I licked his shaft slowly. "Tonight you are mine."

"Yes," he said, his voice husky. "I'm yours."

I could see his ass in the mirror behind us, my hands on his hips as I moved him in and out of my open mouth. "I want to watch," I said, moving his body slightly so I could watch his cock slide in and out of my lips. Seeing us together was intoxicating. I sucked on his shaft and cradled his balls with my hands. His eyes closed, his head rolled back and I saw how his hips pushed into me, his body relaxing and channeling every bit of energy he had into my mouth. I moved faster and faster, pulling him in so deeply I thought I might choke but I wanted to taste him, I needed this.

taken by someone so big and wide. He stayed totally still and I breathed feeling him inside me, this moment, this connection, our bodies fused together.

"You ready," he whispered. "Do you feel this, this energy between us?"

"I feel it. I'm ready," I said, moaning.

Legs still against his chest, he rocked forward, sliding in and out of me. I watched in the mirror, the sight of his cock penetrating me was so erotic, so sexual. I felt the heat building in me way too fast. I moaned as he caressed me from the inside, slowly, deeply.

Then he moved faster, harder.

"More," I whispered.

"Tell me," he said, his voice ragged. I had closed my eyes without realizing it and looked up to see him staring at me, his eyes a mix of lust and need.

"I need more," I said, reaching for him. I opened my legs wider, pulling him on top of me. The weight of him against my clitoris was so intense. He rubbed against me as he pushed inside. I gasped and grabbed his ass wanting him deeper.

"Fuck me," I said, pulling him closer. "Fuck me hard."

I kept my eyes open as he pounded against me, always rubbing against my clit, I could feel the pressure growing.

Then he arched his back, his mouth on my tits, he sucked as he pulled out a bit, then drove into me again. I could feel him controlling the rhythm trying not to move too quickly. Then the energy shifted and I felt my body take control of our pace, with my hands on his ass, I pulled him towards me, legs locking around his waist. "Like this," I said, rocking against him, arching up, my body tensing up with every push.

Again and again he hammered against me until I felt the shaking in my core and an orgasm rocked through me so hard I screamed, my fingers digging into his back. He kept moving. I gasped laughing. "Did you, did you?"

"Not yet," he said smiling. "But you are making it difficult." He flipped me over. My ass up, he raised my body up and slid inside me from behind. I opened up so easily my body still tingling from the orgasm. I watched in the mirror feeling myself grow even wetter if that was possible, my tits hard, and my breathing shallow. I watched as his rock hard cock slid in and out of me, his hands on my waist.

"Tell me want you want," he said, as he pulled my hips back and forth sliding me on his shaft.

"I want to feel you in deep, I want to see your gorgeous cock," I said, moving with him faster and faster. He leaned over me, his hand reaching around my waist and rubbing against my pussy as he pushed inside of me. He kissed my back as his cock slid inside me, and his fingers against me.

Faster, faster, again, and again I felt myself coming. "Again," I said, "I'm coming again." I took a breath willing my body to slow.

"On the floor," I said, leaning forward so he slid out of me.

He nodded and lifted me up sliding his cock into my pussy. I gasped at the sensation. I could feel the orgasm teasing me. I was at the brink of coming again. Carrying me to the soft white carpet directly in front of the mirror, he dropped to the floor, raising me up for a moment only to slide me back onto his throbbing shaft. My legs wrapped around him, my breasts pressed against him, our mouths on each other we rocked back and forth. We were so close to the mirror that I felt as though I were outside of myself watching us make love.

Was this making love? The thought flew through my mind so quickly I pushed it aside. This was sex, raw and powerful, this was fucking. This was beautiful, fucking beautiful. We were making love, the most fucking beautiful love I'd ever felt.

"You're in control, love," he said. "Take me. I'll come

with you this time."

And I felt the energy shift back to me. I moved against him the way I wanted to. Eyes open, I watched us in the mirror. I had never felt so intimate and so fucking hot at the same time. I pushed him back so I could straddle him, my tits dangling over his body. When I wanted to I lifted up long enough for him to take me in his mouth before sliding my legs around him again, feeling the whole of him inside me.

"No stopping this time," I said, my voice ragged and deep with need. "No stopping, do you feel this? Do you feel this?" I heard my voice and wondered who I was, I sounded so out of control but I wasn't self-conscious. I felt like a woman about to lose her mind.

Theo moaned, his eyes closing and back arching. His hand gripped my hips as I rode him harder, faster, and then the waves started. I screamed arching back as he grabbed my hips and pulled me deeper onto his cock, I could feel him throbbing and pulsing inside me in waves that seemed to go on and on. We collapsed against each other, his cock inside me shaking, my pussy throbbing and aching. I collapsed against his chest.

"Nobody has ever made me feel like that," I said. "How did you do that?"

His Five Night Stand

"Me?" he said. "That was you, all you." Kisses on my face, my neck, I moaned as he pulled out of me. I felt an emptiness without him inside. He pulled me close, nestling my head against his neck and kissed my forehead.

"So, that's night three," I said, feeling a mix of regret and grief that I couldn't bear. "I can't imagine what you are going to do to me on nights four and five. I have to tell you I think I'm cured."

"The night's not over," he said, rolling on top of me.

"I seriously need a minute," I said, laughing. "As much as I'd love to do that again."

His arms on either side of me, his cock erect above me. "I'll give you a minute," he said, winking. "But only a minute." He lay down beside me. "One. Two. Three. A minute is sixty seconds you know . . ."

"You're counting," I laughed.

"I don't want this night to be over," he said, his voice serious.

"Then don't let it end," I said, turning to look at him. Not in the mirror this time, but really looked at him. His pale blue eyes on me, his lips parted as if he wanted to say something in response. A thousand things ran through my mind. Maybe we could break the rules. Would a sixth or seventh night be that bad? Did he feel the energy I felt?

Surely this was more than just an experiment, but I had to be okay with things the way they were, right?

"Hey, you made the rules and I agreed to them," I said, running my fingers through his hair. "At least we have two more nights. I'll take whatever I can get."

"Yes, two more," he said, a weariness in his voice that I didn't understand.

* * * *

We fell asleep and I woke to his lips on my neck gently kissing me. Our bodies still slick with sweat, he took my hand and wordlessly led me across the room toward his bathroom. The room was all black and white tiles with an oversized shower and bright chrome fixtures. It had clearly been updated in the last few years unlike my antique bath.

"It's late for a shower," I whispered.

"I want you in water," he said, opening a drawer he took out a book of matches and lit a series of candles on the black tile countertop. He turned on the shower and dimmed the lights. Steam filled the room. It was so sensual and sexy I didn't want to speak.

Theo took my hand.

"This way, love," he said, opening the wide glass door. We stepped into the shower. My body ached from wanting him, it was so beautiful and so gut wrenchingly sexy. I could feel myself growing wet before a drop of water hit my skin.

Theo kissed me softly as the warm water covered us. "You are mixing me up Callie," he said, his tongue pushing into my mouth, his hands moving to my tits and between my legs.

"Is that a good thing?" I asked between kisses. "It feels good to me."

"I want to know you," he said. "I want to know every part of you. Where you spend your days, what you dream at night."

"I dream of this," I said, grabbing his hand and sliding his fingers between my legs.

He laughed and slid out of me. "I'm serious," he said, taking my face in his hands. "I know you are a designer, an artist. I've seen what you've done with your apartment; you have a gift for finding the soul of a space. I want to know more about you."

"You want to know about my childhood?" I giggled. "This is sounding very serious."

Something flashed across his face. "You're right, I'm sorry. The rules."

"I don't care about the rules," I said, grasping his hands. "I barely know you but in a few nights you've made me feel sexier and more powerful than I've ever felt in my life. I don't care about the rules, Theo. Just love me again, please."

He moaned softly and pulled me towards him, his mouth against mine, his hardness growing as he pressed against me. Then he turned and grabbed the shower head, unclipping it from the wall and moving the spray up and down my body.

"Spread your legs," he whispered to me.

I stepped away from him and spread my legs as he let the water pulse across my body. He moved the spray down my body as he adjusted the pressure to a slow pulse. Then he held the pulsing water against my crotch. I gasped as the vibration moved through me. The steady pulsing teasing me, I moaned and he slipped his arms around me holding me up as he played with the water adjusting the speed from a slower pulse to a heavier pulse, the water vibrated against my clit.

I moaned as the humming against my clit continued. I could feel a wave of pleasure building inside me.

I grabbed the shower head from him and rotated on the tiles, legs spread I bent over holding the throbbing water to my pussy. "Come inside me," I begged. "Come inside me, please."

His Five Night Stand

I felt his hands on my hips and his enormous cock pushing inside me. He spread me open as I held the water against my clit, he pushed in and out and we moaned together as I adjusted the water to a faster rate. He pumped into me again and again until the building orgasm inside me could no longer be contained.

"Now, now, now," I screamed holding the water against my shuddering body as he drove into me so deep I almost cried out in a wave of pleasure and pain. I felt him shaking and shuddering as he came inside me, collapsing over my back. I almost fell to the floor, but he caught me and I dropped the shower head. He spun me around and we stood there together, our bodies shaking, dripping with sex and water. His mouth against mine, he held me in an embrace as the shaking continued for us both. I knew we had been foolish we hadn't used a condom but it had been impossible to stop. We'd be smarter next time. Already I was aching for the next time.

"That was amazing," I whispered, high on the orgasm, high on feeling uninhibited and loved.

"We are amazing together," he said. "Come back to bed, love." We stepped out of the shower and wrapped ourselves in thick white towels. Hand in hand we walked back to the bed and slipped beneath the covers to sleep.

Emma Thorne

When I awoke at 10:00 a.m., I was alone in Theo's bed.

CHAPTER 18

I don't know what I expected the morning after. Orange juice on a tray, lattes from an impromptu coffee run. For a few moments, I lay perfectly still under the covers and watched light filter in through the translucent white drapes in his room. "Theo?" I called softly. But I knew he wouldn't answer.

Then I saw his note.

Sorry I had to run. I'll be in touch—T

The words I'll be in touch filled me with a sense of dread. I felt cold as I picked up my clothes and slipped on my dress feeling like a college girl on the walk of shame, but there was no shame this time at least until I opened the door. Then there was just embarrassment.

Odessa and Shea sat on the couch, magazines in hand.

"I win," Shea said, turning to high five Odessa. "Up before 11:00 a.m."

"Seriously?" I said, my cheeks burning. Sure I was happy I'd gotten some the night before, but I wasn't ready to share explicit details with the world.

"Don't be embarrassed!" Odessa said, jumping up. "I just got home myself. Theo left for work a few minutes ago.

You just missed him."

"I can't believe I didn't wake up when he left," I said, feeling awkward in my red dress and heels.

"Um . . .?" Shea said, patting the cushion besides her. "Details please."

"Details?" I took a seat, not realizing how tired I was until I sat down.

"They didn't have actual sex yet Shea, it's only night three," Odessa said.

"No sex?" Shea said. "That's freakin' tragic."

"Umm . . ." I said, uncertain how to handle this conversation. Theo had mentioned rules, but he had bent them with me. Surely he had done the same with other women.

Odessa's eyes widened. "Wait, did you have actual sex?"

"Well . . ."

"And by sex we mean penis in vagina," Shea said.

"Seriously Shea," Odessa said, rolling her eyes.

"What? That is how people have sex you know," Shea said. "Sometimes, of course there is vagina and vagina, or penis, vagina, vagina. I could go on."

"We had sex, last night and there was only one penis and one vagina," I said, heat building as I remembered all the different positions. My body ached and throbbed at the memory of Theo pulsing and pushing inside me, but I wasn't sore I wanted more. I hoped he would get in touch soon. I knew I probably needed a day to catch up on sleep and let my muscles rest. Still I would have closed his bedroom door and fallen back into bed with him in a minute if he had shown up and taken my hand.

"You seriously had sex in his bed," Odessa said.

"In his bed, on the floor, against the wall, in front of the mirror . . ." I giggled.

"You and Theo," Odessa said, eyes wide with what looked like disbelief.

"What are you not getting?" Shea said.

"It's just this is a serious deviation from his pattern. What else happened last night?" Odessa turned to me, her eyes in investigation mode.

"I don't know. We went to The Cloud Room downtown?"

"He took you out somewhere?" Odessa said, mouth gaping.

"And then we decided it was time to have sex, so we came back to his place." I couldn't help but smile remembering our conversation. I had wanted him so much. I had chosen this, asked for what I wanted and I wanted more.

"Oh my," Odessa said, standing. She ran her fingers through her long dark hair. "This could be bad, or it could be good. I don't know."

"What is bad?" I asked, my stomach tightening. "There was nothing bad about last night."

"Again, details on the sex, please," Shea said, sounding exasperated.

"Theo has a program," Odessa said, standing. She moved to the center of the room under the chandelier holding a coffee cup in her hand. "The nights are always the same, he moves progressively towards sex, but never ever wavers. Night one, two, three. It's his thing."

"I don't get it. You didn't have sex?" Shea said, disappointed.

"They have different kinds of sex every night," Odessa said. "But he saves it for the last night. The last night is when he finally makes love to a woman. It's the last thing. And then it's over."

"We most definitely deviated from the plan," I said.

Shea handed me a cup of coffee. "You should drink this. You are probably still drunk on sex. Coffee will wake you up." She stood. "I'm out. I'm calling Troy and tell him to come home from work and take me to bed now. Later girls."

"Later," Odessa said, as Shea left the room.

Then Odessa turned and looked at me. Her expression stunned, she wrinkled her brow as she shook her head.

"I don't get it," I said. "Is there something wrong with what we did?"

"No," Odessa said, smiling. "Maybe it's the opposite. Maybe Theo is happy with you. He never makes love to a woman on the third night and I've never seen him take a woman into his own bed. Clearly he sees you differently than other women. I was actually hoping he might."

"He doesn't have sex with women in that room? I thought he was joking when he told me that."

"Honey," Odessa said. "I haven't even been in that room. When Theo moved into that room it became his space. His sanctuary."

"And he let me inside," I said, my voice soft.

"He let you in honey," Odessa said, sitting next to me on the couch. "I just hope you two know what you are doing."

"We are two people who have no commitment to each other outside of enjoying the moment, taking pleasure in each other. We agreed to this. We have a plan."

"I have known Theo for years," Odessa said. "Maybe

you aren't the only one who is getting healed from a broken heart."

My heart hammered at Odessa's words. Was she right? Maybe this was something more? Theo was the one who set the rules. I agreed, and I was fine with five nights and goodbye. I knew what I was getting out of this agreement. I was getting great sex and a sense of myself again.

"You know what, maybe it means something, maybe it's nothing," Odessa said. "I don't want to stress you out and it's not my business. I'm sure he's fine."

"Right, I'm sure," I said.

"There are worse things than making a man like Theo Manhattan happy."

CHAPTER 19

I spent the day at my apartment sleeping off the sex of the night before. I could close my eyes and imagine Theo in bed beside me, his hands and mouth on my body and finally the feeling of his cock inside me. Sex was different with Theo. From the moment I felt the tip of him against me it was as if my body opened up for him, to feel him sliding inside me, pushing against my soft wet walls.

And we had two more nights together, I told myself as I drifted in and out of sleep. I would have Theo again, I smiled. I would take my two nights. I would take whatever I could get. He was teaching me about pleasure but I didn't feel like a student. I felt like his equal. I understood now what I wanted, how to ask for it. I sighed and rolled over glancing at my door, wishing he was standing outside.

That's when I saw the white card on the floor.

My heart hammered in my chest. Night four. He had to have come home from work while I was sleeping. Maybe he had knocked and I hadn't heard.

I climbed out of bed, grabbing a blanket and wrapping it around my pajama clad body as I moved to the door.

I lifted the card and switched on a light to read. Night

had fallen while I slept.

It's best if we end our agreement with Night 3. You are a beautiful woman and you no longer need me to heal your heart. I wish you all the best and will remember every moment we shared. T.

End our agreement.

It's best.

His words hit me like a punch in the stomach.

No. No. No.

I held the note and turned in circles, my vision blurring with tears.

I would not allow a man to make me cry, not again. I would not be that heartbroken girl for another moment.

But Theo's words were so familiar to me. I knew that tone, that feeling of being dismissed.

Who did Theo think he was anyway, breaking things off with a notecard? What kind of a person did that after all we'd shared?

But this wasn't a relationship. This was a five night stand, his five night stand.

It wasn't as if this was the end of some grand romance, right?

I paced across the hardwood, arms crossed, hands shaking as I held that expensive fucking notecard.

His Five Night Stand

Why was I so angry? So Hurt? It was just sex. Uncomplicated, amazing, incredibly hot sex. I had known it would end and so what if it ended on night three instead of five? This was the point of a one night, two night, whatever night stand, right? Have sex, fuck your brains out don't get attached. And I hadn't gotten attached so why did I feel queasy and why did my mind feel like a top spinning searching for a reason that Theo would have ended our engagement early.

I sunk to the ground beside my futon leaning against the makeshift mattress where Theo had repeatedly rocked my world. Wait a minute, where I had rocked my own world, I reminded myself. Theo had told me that I was the one in control of my own pleasure. I understood now that if I wanted to feel something I needed to want it, to ask for it, scream for it sometimes.

I actually giggled at that thought. I had come a long way from my nights of silent love making with Henry.

Odessa had warned me that Theo had rules. Hell, so had Theo himself. Maybe we had broken too many of his special rules. And maybe it didn't really matter because it was over and the sooner I accepted that and moved on the better off I could be.

"I'm not attached," I whispered, my eyes filling with

tears. "I'm not attached because it was just a fling, nothing more."

I sat on the hardwood floor fighting the urge to get up and pound on Theo's door and demand he tell me we were done in person. I needed to talk to him. Even if it really was over, which was totally okay because I was cool with this whole situation, I just needed to speak to him, to hear his voice. I needed more than his handwriting on a note card.

But then I thought it through. What would I say to him anyway if he opened his door? "Um, sorry, you owe me two more nights?" I laughed out loud at the thought. Theo owed me nothing. I barely knew him.

But his body belongs with you, a voice inside my head whispered. You fit together, you crave him and you will forever.

No. I argued with myself. My body craves a lover. I had been with Henry for years and never felt the way I'd felt with Theo, but Theo had taught me about pleasure. I laid down on my futon, eyes closed, clutching the note to my chest. Was I stupid enough to believe that a bunch of orgasms added up to something that felt like love?

But it had felt like love. Feeling him inside me had felt like love and now the idea of missing a moment with him made me ache more than my grief for Henry.

His Five Night Stand

"Pathetic," I whispered, eyes closed. "You don't need Theo. You don't need Henry. You will find another lover. You know what you need now. You know how to ask for what you want."

Theo was not a relationship, he was a lover, probably my first real lover actually and now he was part of my past. He was a memory, a beautiful memory that I would hold until I took my next lover.

My eyes snapped open.

Had I just thought about the concept of taking a lover?

Theo had changed me. I wanted him, I wanted him badly but I no longer felt totally broken.

Eventually I slept. I dreamt of him again. It was the same dream as before. I wandered down a dark hallway only half dressed, wearing a black button down shirt and nothing else searching for Theo.

He found me and pushed me against a wall. "Again," he whispered.

At the sound of his voice I grew wet, I wanted him immediately.

Then his hands were under my clothes, and I felt him harden as he lifted me up and easily slid inside.

"Again and again," he said.

In my dream we fucked against the wall until I felt the

familiar wave of an orgasm rocking through me. I awoke gasping and moaning, my pussy wet and throbbing with pleasure.

I closed my eyes trying to forget that the only place I would make love to him now was in my dreams. It would have to be enough.

CHAPTER 20

The next morning, I lay in bed staring at the plaster ceiling overhead. Sunlight filtered through the long white curtains at the window. I listened to the hum of traffic from the streets outside; a siren rang in the distance.

For a moment I felt a sinking sensation in my belly. Disappointment. Rejection. There would be no notecard from Theo under my door. It was over and the sooner I accepted the situation the better.

I sat up in bed and stretched taking in the details of my tiny apartment. There was the beach scene above my bed, my antique table, and mercury candlesticks. I made my bed that morning, taking care to pull the comforter straight. My apartment wasn't full of expensive pieces of furniture but the sum of its parts came together in a way that was more beautiful and peaceful than any room I'd ever shared with Henry.

Theo had complimented me on the way I'd made the space my own. I smiled at the memory. He was right. I was proud of my little home. It was beautiful and it was mine.

The apartment reminded me of how much I enjoyed taking a space and finding its personality. Using the natural

213

light of a room to draw out hidden beauty. Discovering the potential of an overlooked piece of furniture, or how a grouping of dissimilar items could come together into a symphony of design.

For the first time in almost a week I noticed my leather portfolio on the bottom shelf of my bookcase. I hadn't looked at it since the break up after that long day at work.

I picked up the portfolio and opened it on my antique table, spreading out the drawings I'd recently added for the Smith Tower contract. I'd worked on the presentation for two weeks straight. I'd barely slept, but it had been worth it. I was so proud of what I'd created. The color palate a tribute to the weather and sky, cool blues and grays mixed with ivory and accents of bright white. The floor to ceiling windows obscured by nothing aside from a custom designed privacy window I'd placed in the bath. I'd wanted to create a sense of the sea besides the sky, an oasis, a retreat. It was beautiful and it was all mine, my creativity, my vision. I had been so caught up in the drama of being dumped I'd forgotten to feel proud of myself

"Tell me what you want," I heard Theo's voice in my memory.

He'd been asking me how I wanted to be loved, but truly there was so much more to that question. What did I want in my life? Did I want a job where I felt used and exploited? Was I okay with having my work stolen from me and presented as somebody else's?

"Hell no, that's not okay," I said, my pulse racing. I pulled up a folding chair and spread out all of the material in my portfolio. I was missing some key samples. I had never made it a priority to showcase my work. That needed to change. If I was going to quit my job and find something new I really needed to spend some time preparing.

My hand froze over the sketches. Quit my job.

Had I really just thought about walking away from the firm that was supposedly giving me my big break? Didn't I need to pay my dues?

I thought of that last breakfast with Henry, the way he'd counseled me to be confident but not too confident. Take credit, but not too much. He had warned me not to get cocky, to remember that I wasn't the one in charge.

How had I spent so much time with a man who basically told me it was acceptable to be treated like a doormat?

I picked up the drawings and stacked them, my hands shaking. My agreement with Theo was over, it was time for me to dig in and take responsibility for my life, to take charge and ask for what I wanted and needed. I would use the weekend to go into the office and put my portfolio together. It would take a couple days to get all the images I needed, and then I'd be ready to quit. And as much as I wanted to depart in some dramatic righteous scene, I needed my job. I would prepare first. My mind was made up. I was going to ask the universe for what I wanted and I'd accept nothing less.

CHAPTER 21

I woke up early on Saturday, ready to go into the office and start pulling pics for my portfolio when my cell phone rang.

"Cal."

There was only one person who called me Cal. I walked across my apartment standing in front of the window that faced the alley, paying attention to how my body felt. My heart rate neutral, in fact I wasn't sure I felt anything at all.

"Are you there?" Henry asked, his voice uncertain.

I enjoyed that moment.

"What do you want, Henry?"

"Hey, you're there and sound good, I wanted. I thought . . ."

For once I didn't chatter and fill the silence. I let him hang there blowing in the wind.

"I thought we could talk," he said.

"About what?"

"About life, about how you are? About how crazy things got between us," he laughed.

I did not. "How crazy things got between us."

"Yeah, it's just I miss you." His voice sounded thick

with something. Sadness. Loneliness. In spite of all that neutrality, hearing that emotion felt like a punch in the chest.

"You miss me," I repeated, feeling the familiar need to comfort him rising up. "What does that even mean? It's been a week Henry."

"Coffee," he said. "Meet me for a drink, something, anything. Whatever makes you comfortable? I need to see you."

He needed me.

"Coffee."

And that is how I found myself having coffee with my ex about a week after he'd broken my heart.

* * * *

We met downtown near the old condo. Henry suggested the location, a small coffee shop where we used to get crepes on the weekend. It was later in the day so we'd missed the morning brunch crowd.

Henry sat at a small cafe table near the front door, a series of black and white photos by a local artist hanging on the wall behind him. We'd sat at this table many times before always ordering the same thing. Non-fat lattes, since Henry felt we should watch our fat intake, and two different crepes. He always picked the order looking for the perfect balance of sweet and savory and of course good nutrition.

Henry's eyes lit up when he saw me; he stood awkwardly, his mouth turning into an uncertain smile. He had circles under his eyes and his dark brown hair looked unkempt. He wore a grey suit and a white button down, no tie. He looked wrinkled and tired. It was odd but instead of looking messy it made him look more normal, more approachable.

As I walked toward that tiny cafe table I found myself remembering the boy I'd fallen in love with all those years ago.

"Hello Henry," I said, smiling in spite of everything that had happened.

"You look beautiful," he said, reaching to pull out a chair.

I stopped him. "I got this." I scooted the chair in myself. "And you're serious. You're really going to start by telling me I look beautiful. That's your lead."

"But you do," he said, his face crestfallen. He had already ordered me a latte. I could tell from the foam it was non-fat milk. My heart rate increased but not because I was nervous anymore, I was suddenly annoyed, very annoyed.

"Thanks,'" I said, taking a sip of the coffee to be polite. Old habits die hard. "So, why are we here Henry?"

"I thought we might be able to spend time together."

"What does Sophia think about that?"

"Sophia doesn't matter."

"I don't understand. She didn't work out and now you're calling me?" I put down my coffee cup the non-fat completely tasteless.

"No, she did work out, she could have . . . I mean . . ." He ran his fingers through his hair. "I screwed everything up. Sophia and I drove down the coast late this week."

"Seriously? You took her on our trip?"

"Sorry, maybe I shouldn't have told you that. It's just we had reservations, some were not refundable." He said it with such confidence.

"Yes, a shame. God Forbid you lose your deposit, Henry."

"I'm screwing this all up."

"You're fine, go on," I said, leaning back in my chair.

"It's just the more time we spent together the more I realized how good things were with us. I made a horrible mistake letting you go, Cal. You have no idea how much I regret it, I regret everything. I want you back."

I looked into his dark brown eyes. They were so familiar. Here was the face of the man I had loved for five years of my life and he was finally speaking the words that

I'd dreamed about. He wanted me back, the Sophia experiment was over. I could have my old life back. I just needed to say yes.

The problem was, I no longer wanted it.

"Things weren't that good between us Henry," I said, taking two packs of sugar and pouring them into my latte.

"Sure they were," he said, reaching across the table to take my hand. "I know you are angry, but you know it's true. You and I just work. We never fight, we enjoy each other's company, we have fun together. I'm an asshole, that's what happened to us."

"True." I shrugged. He had a point.

Something flashed in his eyes and I wondered if he had expected me to soothe him and assure him he was wrong, but a lot had changed over the past ten days. I looked at his hand on top of mine and I thought about how the old Callie would have held his hand tightly grateful for something familiar, something safe.

I had wanted so badly to be chosen by him, but what I realized now is that I needed to choose myself.

I slid my hand out from under his. "We are over Henry."

"Don't say that. We had five good years together, you just don't shut something like that off."

"You already did," I laughed. "And you have to believe me when I say it's okay. I understand now that we weren't that good together. Someday you'll believe me."

His brow furrowed, his breath short and intense. "You've found someone else, is that it?"

"No. I'm not with anyone. I haven't found anyone but myself, Henry. You picked me all those years ago and I was so grateful, so happy to be approved by you. And then you changed your mind and it crushed me."

"I'm sorry, you have no idea." He looked so pained, his hands reaching again across the table.

"It's okay, you were attracted to Sophia. I don't fault you, she's hot and we had fun together, but let's be honest it wasn't like we had sparks."

"There were sparks."

I raised my eyebrows. "You picked me Henry but I never picked you." I took a gulp of my now sweetened latte and stood up. "And I'm not going back to you because it's familiar, or it's easy. I'd rather be alone."

"Cal, we can be better together. We can find the spark. We just need to try."

"No, we can't," I said. "And you know what? I don't drink non-fat lattes. I actually hate them. I always did. Before you order for a woman next time, find out what she really wants."

I kissed his cheek and pulled an envelope with a reimbursement check out of my purse, placing it on the table. I had written the check that morning after I'd agreed to the coffee date. "This is only a portion, but I'll be paying you back in full for your loan," I said.

"It wasn't a loan," he said, pushing the envelope towards me.

I shrugged. "Goodbye, Henry. Good luck."

I walked out of the coffee shop and I didn't look back.

CHAPTER 22

Henry and I were over, this was true. But this time I was walking away. I was choosing a different life not running away with my head hanging.

Each step away from him felt like a movement towards my new life. Ironically it had started with the end of not one but two relationships. First Henry and then Theo. I had never felt so inspired by so much loss.

It was late Saturday afternoon so the financial part of the city was almost deserted. The sky was robin's egg blue. Puffy white clouds billowed overhead. It was a gorgeous Seattle day. I wore a yellow sundress with sandals, my hair loose. I didn't need my cardigan so I wrapped it around my shoulders.

I decided to walk through the city and then grab the train to the office at Lake Union. I'd brought my portfolio with me. The plan was to spend a few hours gathering images from key projects. I'd print them off-site so no one could accuse me of stealing office supplies or something ridiculous like that.

I felt exhilarated walking through the city. My heart felt big and strong thinking about my life and where it might be going. I had a place to live, I knew I needed to make a change at work and I no longer doubted that I would. I felt inspired and un-stuck. I didn't have a lover but I'd learned that the only way I was ever going to get what I wanted in life was to ask for it.

"I expect a wonderful life," I whispered to myself, waiting at a stop light near the art museum. A crowd of people following a tour guide holding an umbrella in the air gathered around me. I expect love. I expect passion. I expect satisfaction.

I rattled off the things I wanted and needed, never realizing where I was going until I stood underneath the neon sign that Shea had described to me that night in the laundry room not so long ago.

Blue and White neon—a skyline of NYC in downtown Seattle.

Manhattan Galleries.

The signed buzzed and flickered overhead.

I looked inside the large windows. A series of paintings hung in the front room—beautiful poppies in shades of sunlight. The walls were white like Theo's bedroom, the ceiling high. Through a wide archway I saw a brass sculpture on a black pillar. It was of a woman kneeling, her hands across her belly with an expression that could only be called joy.

And as if on cue Theo walked into frame.

He crossed the room, his face tense but invigorated. An elegant elderly woman in a pale blue suit followed him as he walked through the room. His hands gesturing as he walked, he was sharing something with her, his passion for his art clear in the intensity of his gaze. I stood perfectly still transfixed.

What did I want out of life?

I was looking right at him.

I walked inside.

You get the life you ask for. It was time to start talking.

* * * *

I walked straight up to Theo. He stood, his back towards me holding some papers in his hand. The woman exited out the front door behind me, bells ringing as the door closed.

"Hello there," I said, my heart pounding with excitement. What if he rejected me? What if he didn't? It didn't matter anymore. I wasn't going to let fear stop me from asking for what I wanted in life. I was going to be brave.

Theo turned, his eyes widened when he saw me and he opened his mouth as if to say something, but instead he was silent. He closed his mouth and swallowed.

"You could start with hello," I said. "I won't bite."

"I'm sorry," he said. "You surprised me, you always do." The last phrase he muttered a little more softly.

"Will you show me your art?" I asked, drinking in his face, his pale blue eyes. My gaze drifted down his body to his beautiful hands, the hands that I had grown to love on my body in just a few brief nights. "I want to see your sculptures." My heart pounded against my chest and my body flared with heat. The slight chill from the afternoon breeze outside had faded. I was now officially hot blooded.

"Follow me," he said. We moved to the back room, past the sculpture of the woman in the center of the room. Smaller pieces flanked the walls. They were all women in varying poses. "I don't have many pieces on display right now, I am actually rotating out this series now. I have a buyer, the woman who just left . . ."

"They are lovely," I said, my gaze moving from sculpture to sculpture. He'd clearly used the same model for all the different pieces, her expression changing from pose to pose. Sitting down she gazed skyward her face wrinkled with laughter. There she sat on a chair her smile strained with unspoken tension. There were so many different moods. Anger. Sadness. Joy. Rapture. He had captured this woman's soul.

As I walked towards the sculpture in the center of the room I knew without asking who she was. The pivotal sculpture was larger than the rest, lit by a warm yellow light overhead. Naked, the woman's eyes were closed her smile serene, content. She looked like a woman with a precious secret, arms crossed, her hands rested on her belly protectively, maternally. I gasped as I understood all too quickly how much Theo had lost.

"She was pregnant," I said, turning to look at him. "This is Grace, the woman you loved. You lost them both."

He paled even as he stood in the warm sunlight. He inhaled and looked towards the ceiling breathing slowly. His eyes meeting mine, his deep beautiful blue eyes filled with a grief and sadness that made me want to pull him into my arms.

So, I did.

"I'm sorry," I said, holding him close. "I'm so sorry, Theo."

"No one knew," he whispered his voice warm against my ear. "It was early and she was so happy. I've never told a soul. Not a single soul."

I leaned back so I could look up into his face. His pale blue eyes wet with tears, his expression raw with grief but also something that looked like relief.

"Your pain is real," I said. "But I want you to know that you can be happy again. You taught me that. I want what we started even if it goes nowhere. I want more days and nights. And I know that you may tell me right now that you have rules to protect your heart and it's really over and that's okay."

He looked startled but still said nothing.

"I want you Theo Manhattan, even if you don't want me." I felt breathless and dizzy, my body thrumming with energy, I felt a rush of adrenaline racing through my body as I realized I was telling the truth. I was prepared to walk away from him forever, but I wasn't going to walk away without asking for what I wanted.

"And you aren't talking," I said. "Are you in shock, do you want me to leave?"

"Don't go," he said, leaning his forehead against mine. "I want you to say it again."

"Say what?"

"Tell me you want me."

"I want you Theo Manhattan. I want you more than I've ever wanted any man in my life. No matter what happens. I'm in."

He breathed deeply and stepped back cradling my face

in his hands.

"I'm not afraid of your heartbreak," I whispered. "I'm not afraid of your dark places." My body tingled with need and possibility. The freedom and power in asking for what I wanted felt so strong, like a drug.

He nodded and exhaled slowly. "Ever since Grace died, I have been able to sculpt nothing but her. Nothing. And today I sold every piece in this collection. I'm done."

"Why would you give them all away?"

"It is time I let her go," he said, his fingers caressing my cheek. "For the first time since she died, I wanted to sculpt something else, I needed to. It's you," he said. "I want you Callie." He pulled me towards him his lips pressing against me with a fierceness and heat.

I could feel how much he wanted me and I moaned softly as I ran my fingers through his hair. We had kissed each other passionately before, but this felt different, there was an intimacy in it, a trust that made my knees weak.

Someone cleared their throat behind us.

We spun around to see the woman in the pale blue suit standing in front of us holding what I now understood was a contract in her hands.

My cheeks burned as I stood there holding Theo's hand, but I wasn't embarrassed being caught in a major

PDA moment. I wanted Theo and this woman clearly knew it, of course we could have been a little more discrete, but all I could think about now was how long we would have to wait until we ripped each other's clothes off.

The woman smiled before she spoke. "Sorry to interrupt but I wanted to get a referral from you, Theo," she said. "I'm looking for a designer to help with the installation at the house."

"Actually," Theo said, putting his arm around me and nudging me slightly. "This is Callie Barron. She has an excellent eye and you should see what she thinks of your space. Callie this is Rose McGuire."

I managed to stay calm and smile as if this were just an ordinary conversation on an ordinary day.

"Ms. Barron." She held out her be-jeweled hand. "It's lovely to meet you my dear. I'd love to have you come to the house to see what you think."

"Of course Ms. McGuire." I shook her hand feeling so nervous I was afraid I might shake. I wasn't sure if it was the energy from the kiss or the realization that possibilities were opening up all around me.

"Call me Rose," she said.

"Or course, Rose."

I was afraid, but it was time to ask life for what I

wanted.

I explained that I didn't have my card but we exchanged information and I agreed to go to Rose's the following evening to see the space and work up some designs for the installation. "I'll give you some of my ideas and if we think we are a good match for each other, we can move forward."

"That sounds lovely. Thank you both." Rose turned and smiled before leaving. "And you make a beautiful couple. It's nice to see you happy, Theo. It's been a while." She winked and then walked away.

Theo snaked his arm around my waist, his mouth against my neck.

"So, do I make you happy?" I whispered.

"You make a few things happy," he whispered pressing his hardening body against mine.

"You realize you have never actually seen my portfolio," I said, leaning against his body. "What if I have no talent?"

"Oh no. Do you have no talent?" He giggled, kissing me softly between sentences.

"Of course I have talent. I have a lot of talent."

"And I believe in you," he said. "If you want this job you can have it. She's going to love your work I just know it."

"And if this turns into a real job," I whispered leaning against his body. "I suppose you'll require a referral fee of some sort?"

"Oh, I don't know," he said. "I seem to remember that you owe me two nights of passion."

"I owe you two nights? Is that how you remember it?"

"I'll give you two nights and as many as you'll have me," he said, his voice suddenly serious.

"Promise me we start tonight."

"I promise," he said. We stood in the center of the gallery, our arms wrapped around each other, our lips fused together. I felt as if we were the only two people in the whole world.

CHAPTER 23

That night, Theo knocked on my door at exactly 8:12 p.m. I remembered because I'd been watching the clock, waiting for him, wishing for time to pass more quickly. When I opened the door he stood outside wearing the same black t-shirt and jeans from the afternoon. I took his hand and pulled him inside my apartment without hesitation.

"Come here you," I said, giggling as I kissed him hungrily, pulling him towards my bed. His hands on the zipper of my sundress his lips on my neck, tongue in my mouth. There was no hesitation this time, no worries.

"I want to make love to you in your bed," he said, stopping to pull the sheets back. "I want to make love to you in these sheets and wake up beside you in the morning and then make love to you again."

"Yes, please," I whispered falling against him. We fell onto the mattress our clothes off in under a minute. My body responded to him so quickly.

"I need you inside me," I said, pulling him towards me. He groaned as I stroked him with my eager hands.

He handed me a condom. I opened it and quickly sheathed him loving the feeling of his hardness in my hands. I felt so in control, so turned on with anticipation and need.

I straddled him, sliding my wetness onto his throbbing shaft, the sensation of him filling me up making me gasp again. I held my breasts in my hands as I rose slowly up and down pushing myself against him and then leaning forward so my breasts hung near his face. His hands reached me, one hand on my ass he held me tight.

"Slowly," he said, his hands brushing against my cheek. "I want to love you like this," he said and arching his back he pushed into me deeper. "I want to feel every part of you.

I moaned as he withdrew and then pushed just inside, stroking the super sensitive place inside of me that I'd felt him finger before. Then we were moving together rocking back and forth in perfect unison. He pushed inside me, always brushing up against that sensitive spot and then sliding deeper, deeper than I'd ever been touched before. I leaned forward my clit rubbing against him as I pushed down on him.

We moaned together, my hands on his chest rubbing his nipples, my mouth on his chest. Then our hands intertwined and we moved together, faster, harder, harder, the moaning grew louder and louder.

"I can't wait, I can't, now, now, now," I gasped, shaking and screaming as an orgasm rocked through my body. His back arching, I felt him throbbing inside me, a sense of filling up that made my orgasm ripple on and on. I collapsed on top of him shaking, his lips on my forehead as I rolled beside him.

His mouth on me, he kissed me slowly, carefully. "No woman has ever made me feel the way you do," his words held a weight, a message. I knew it was deliberate.

I answered him with a kiss. As his lips pressed against mine, I felt my body responding again, his fingers brushing against my throbbing pussy.

"Please," I moaned, unsure if I wanted him to please stop or please keep going.

"Like this," he said, his fingers moving against me in slow circles. It was almost too much to bear my body still ached from coming.

"I can't, I can't," I whispered.

"Yes, you can, softly, just relax."

I closed my eyes and leaned back as he fingered me, my throbbing wet clit aching from the previous orgasm. His mouth on my breast, his fingers coaxed me along slowly, I felt the tingling moving through my whole body.

"I love watching you come," he said. "There is nothing

more erotic than watching you shake and quiver."

"More," I whispered arching against him as the pressure increased, then his fingers were inside me two at a time, his mouth on my breast sucking, biting.

I felt my body tightening, my legs tensing. I opened my eyes and grabbed him with my hands. "With you inside me," I whispered. "Please, now. I want you to feel me shake." I spread my legs apart as he slipped on another condom and climbed on top of me.

We both gasped as our bodies locked together. We rocked back and forth the groaning and moaning coming faster and louder this time. My hands on his ass, I pushed him in arching my back, needing him deeper, his hands on my tits, mouth dropping to suck on my nipples as he pounded against me.

I needed nothing but this. There was nothing but this moment of pleasure, this heat between us, our bodies slick with sweat, my pussy dripping, and his cock hard and throbbing.

"Harder," I gasped. "Fuck me harder."

"What do you want, love?" he asked.

"Fuck me harder."

"I can't hear you."

"Fuck me now, harder, harder," I yelled my voice

unfamiliar to me as he drove into me relentlessly, this feeling of being possessed and taken overwhelming me as I broke open. Shaking and shuddering I moaned as he collapsed on top of me. We lay like that, connected together, the pulsing of our bodies still carrying on even while still.

"That was bloody amazing," he said, nibbling my ear.

I giggled. "You take direction quite well."

"I look forward to more," he said, rolling beside me, his arm slipping easily behind my head.

Suddenly there was a pounding on the wall from the room next door. Odessa. "Keep it down in there you two," she shouted.

We collapsed in a fit of laughter.

"You feel like being quiet, love?" Theo asked nibbling my ear.

"Hell no," I said, standing and walking toward the wall. I spread my legs and parted myself with my fingers rubbing the soft wet part of myself with one hand, the other on my breast. "Get over here, lover," I said, smiling. "Let's wake the neighbors."

And so we did.

About the Author

Emma Thorne's approach to writing romance is that sexy + fun = happily ever after. She lives in Seattle with her smoking hot husband and their two children, a superhero of a little boy, and an adorable baby girl. Emma loves connecting with readers.

Find Emma online!
http://emmathornebooks.com
https://twitter.com/emmathornebooks
https://www.facebook.com/emmathornebooks

Dear Reader,

I hoped you enjoyed Callie and Theo's love story. Writing Book 1 of this series about new lovers and second chances was a ton of fun.

I have a favor to ask. If you have time, please **write a review** for *His Five Night Stand.* I appreciate all feedback. If you do write a review be sure to email me at emmathornebooks@gmail.com so I can send you a personal message to say thank you.

Also, if you want to learn more about the bedroom secrets world and other new series Join my mailing list @ http://eepurl.com/bAf70r for news, free books, and giveaways.

Thank you so much for reading Callie and Theo's story. I hope to share more of the bedroom secrets world with you in the future and other sexy + fun = happily ever after stories.

XO
Emma

Sneak Peek - His Four Poster Bed

Find out the story behind Odessa and Theo's past as The Bedroom Secrets series continues with Odessa's love story in *His Four Poster Bed.*

A sexy bad boy billionaire can turn any woman's life upside down, but when Odessa Starr meets Marco Pranzo, it could mean the end of life as she knows it.

Odessa's passion for her medical career leaves little time for love. An awkward breakup has her swearing off romantic complications, but that New Year's resolution is dead before midnight when she meets Marco. It's more than the cut of his tuxedo and gorgeous blue gray eyes that draw her into his dangerous world. They share an instant connection that could lead to the true love they've both yearned for.

Marco Pranzo wants to change his life and escape the shadow of his family's illegal businesses. Helping the feds build a case against them may ease his conscience, but it also puts his life in danger. To survive he'll have to disappear, and to be with him, Odessa will have to do the same, leaving behind her family, her friends, and the career that she's worked so hard to build. Will she trade in her identity for a lifetime of nights in his four poster bed?

Coming soon!

For updates on publication dates Join my Mailing list: http://eepurl.com/bAf70r

XO
Emma

Printed in Great Britain
by Amazon

42325973R00138